MOLLY FLANAGAN
AND THE
Holy Ghost

For Susan
good luck with
both your poetry
and fiction

Margaret
April 1, 1995

MARGARET SKINNER

MOLLY FLANAGAN
AND THE
Holy Ghost

ALGONQUIN BOOKS OF CHAPEL HILL

1995

Published by
ALGONQUIN BOOKS OF CHAPEL HILL
Post Office Box 2225
Chapel Hill, North Carolina 27515-2225

a division of
WORKMAN PUBLISHING COMPANY, INC.
708 Broadway
New York, New York 10003

Library of Congress Cataloging-in-Publication Data
Skinner, Margaret, 1942–
    Molly Flanagan and the holy ghost / Margaret Skinner.—1st ed.
      p. cm.
    ISBN 1–56512–026–4
    I. Title.
    PS3569.K525M65   1994
    813'.54—dc20   94–35030
                                                CIP

10 9 8 7 6 5 4 3 2 1
First Edition

Many thanks to Louis D. Rubin, Jr., for his counsel and friendship; to Lisa Poteet for her advice and support; and to my friends and family who have offered encouragement and good cheer, especially Sally Shelton, Sally Johnson, Edie Caywood, June Green, Betty and Wade Harrison, Jim Gordon, my husband, J. B. Skinner, and our sons, Jim, Tom, and Will Skinner.

FOR MARGARET SCOTT PENDERGRAST

MOLLY FLANAGAN
AND THE
Holy Ghost

PRELUDE

"*Tres. Quattuor.*" Nat pivoted and headed the pushmower straight down the row, spewing grass that stuck to his sweaty legs like green hair. Molly sat down beside her father on the glider under the shade of the stringbean tree; his face was red and his blue shirt spotted with sweat. He and Nat took turns with the pushmower, five rows up and back—*Decem*—then they'd switch off.

Six-year-old Molly was not allowed to cut grass and held the lowly job of water girl. Back and forth, she fetched big jars of ice water for her father and brother and wondered how the yard might look if they scalloped the edges, or cut along the perimeter, making smaller and smaller rectangles until they ended up in the middle. She'd forgotten to bring water for herself and was thirsty, but her father began reading from Bulfinch's *Mythology* and, riveted by the story of Mercury, she sweated and licked salt from her lips. Her father flicked a dirt dauber from the book that seemed to buzz with the feats of gods and goddesses and Molly wished she were one of them. If she were a goddess she'd cut the grass in zigzags and drink ice water until she froze.

The blades of the mower clattered as Nat pushed toward the glider and stopped for a gulp of water. "*Quinque,*" he said, apologetically. He was only ten, but worked as hard as her father so he could get back to the Bulfinch they were both reading, Nat selfishly to himself, her father aloud so that Molly could hear. Nat's place in the book was marked with a yellow gum wrapper, her father's with a silver bookmark. Nat turned up his jar, letting two big cubes slide into his mouth. He puffed cold air like the Old North Wind. "How far did you get?" he asked, nodding toward the book.

"Old Swifty," said her father, as if he recalled Mercury as his closest boyhood friend. "One of the great ones."

Molly's feet itched and she rubbed them back and forth across the nut grass, wondering how it might feel to run so fast you could fly. "Spread your toes," her father said, motioning toward her right foot, and she did that as he peered down, pressing his glasses closer to his eyes. He patted her foot, then dusted his hands on his pants. "Athlete's foot," he observed.

Molly knew that owning only one athlete's foot would do her no good and she stuck her left foot up in front of his face. "This one, too?"

"Yes, that one, too. Athlete's foot." His voice was godlike with the proclamation. Her father was the wisest man she knew and famous for knowing all about sports and athletes. As a young man he'd beaten all comers in the fifty-yard dash and just this past spring picked the winner of the Kentucky Derby. He was tall and wiry, and she imagined him as an Olympian.

"You need foot powder," he said. "And dry your feet after you run. It's a battle that takes a long time to win, so you'd better get on with it. Do it at least three times a day. Remember—three times a day."

Her athlete's feet burned as she envisioned her own head crowned with a laurel wreath. Running three times a day was a lot even with gifted feet, but developing herself into a famous track star *would* take a long time. Suddenly the new-mown grass looked like a green track groomed just for an Olympian. Molly wriggled her toes and took off running.

She sprinted to the creosote posts sunk for her trapeze, jumped up and touched the bar just to prove she could, and ran back again, her pigtails flapping like wings.

"Wait a minute," said her father. "Slow down. It's too hot to run."

"It's dumb," said Nat, sucking ice.

"Dumb because *you* don't have athlete's feet," said Molly, looking scornfully at his old tennis shoes.

Nat put an ice cube on top of his head and let it melt down his face. "Dad, she just doesn't damn *get* it."

"I can see that." He said nothing more, not about Molly's feet or even about Nat's cussing.

Miscues and misunderstandings. Getting things right didn't seem possible, but still she kept trying. She'd let go of one dream, then take up with another. On a dark foggy morning— after flying high as a circus star in her dream the night before— she hung upside down on the trapeze. Her mother, father, and Nat were not yet awake. She wanted very much to skin-the-cat but, wondering why it was called that in the first place, became worried sick over all the cats in the world and felt powerless to perform. She'd hung there thinking for a long time, her head heavy as a bowl of blood, when suddenly she saw Nat slip out of the house and quietly close the back door. The flashlight tied to his waist lit the grass around his feet and he walked within a circle of light.

Nat looked out of focus and she thought maybe the smell of the pine tar caused her eyes to blur, though when she stood right side up, far away from the creosote posts, her eyes often blurred. Nat unlatched the gate and swung through. He shined his light down the gravel driveway, then turned it off. Forgetting cats, Molly dropped to the ground and quietly followed Nat out of the yard and down the street.

Nothing seemed right about his sneaking away from the house or her spying on him, but she trailed him anyhow. The sky began to lighten and she darted from bush to bush so that Nat would not see her in the drifting fog. She rounded the corner and caught sight of him crossing the field, heading determinedly toward the bayou.

"If you go far enough in there you'll see Hell," was what he'd said the night before. "If he's down there, I'll see him."

"I would never look at the Devil," she'd said to him. "If he came near me, I'd fly away."

"I didn't say 'Devil.' If I saw the Devil I'd be scared shitless." Lately Nat had started cussing and just couldn't seem to stop. When he talked about the tunnel that led underground from the bayou wall, to God only knows where, his face glowed red and his mouth slid into a horrible bright smile. Long ago her father declared the bayou off-limits, but Nat had pretended he didn't remember when Molly reminded him.

Nat maneuvered through the Johnson grass and down the

bayou wall. He didn't see her as she hunkered behind the concrete bridge rail, peering down at him. He started chucking rocks that rang like hammers when they hit inside the tunnel. A bat flew out and quickly disappeared before Molly could get scared. But she shuddered hard when a snake slithered out of the tunnel and into the brown water, an evil black creature as long as anything in the world.

She stood up and looked all around her, afraid of more snakes. She thought Nat would see her and be mad that she'd followed him, but just then he entered the tunnel and never looked back. Fear shadowed her like somebody lonesome.

Molly walked to the field, sat on the ground away from the Johnson grass and waited for Nat to come back. Slowly the sun burned away the fog and the putrid smell from the bayou water.

The field of dry grass looked stiff and dead in the morning rays as if burned at the roots from the fires of Hell beneath it. The ground was littered with trash. She slapped at the bugs crawling on her legs and tried not to think about Nat meeting the Devil face-to-face. She almost walked home to tell her parents that he was down there and in danger, but her father called people who tattled "tissy brissers" and she didn't want to be one. She picked up a book of matches from the scrub grass and held it tightly in her hand. Waiting for Nat to come back seemed like a thousand hours.

If her mother or father came looking for them, they'd ask where Nat was and Molly wouldn't know what to say. And anyhow, they'd never believe he'd gone to Hell. She struck a match and with it burned away the thought of tattling on him.

One by one she struck more matches when suddenly the grass caught fire and she was stomping at it.

The flames spread and quickly engulfed the field. She ran back and forth in a panic and then Nat's blackened face and shining green eyes came crashing through the Johnson grass. He hollered and ran toward her, a wild shape-shifting Devil's boy, and Molly was frightened and cried out, for she couldn't yet know that Nat was a fervent and dogged crusader led underground not by the Devil, but by his own sacred mission to spring Grandfather Ignatius "Nate" Flanagan from Hell.

Then the siren blared and through the smoke a fire truck pulled up. Neighbors dressed in bathrobes began to come out of their houses. Molly was in a daze while streams of water rained on the field. The smoke billowed, then faded and died.

When questioned by their father, Nat kept quiet about Molly starting the fire, but from that time on he cussed even more earnestly and often. Molly figured the Devil's words were written on the walls of the underworld and had stuck to Nat like sludge when he crawled through it on his belly.

Soon after the snakes came. And while she didn't then have the wherewithal to understand about Nat or Hell or other things that kept her stirred up, she always knew that the fire of her own setting had run the snakes out of the high grass and into her dreams.

PART ONE

Chapter ONE

Now and again the Flanagans changed places, moving around
the square table like pieces on a board game. When she was six
she had sat in her father's place; at nine, in her mother's. Molly
was almost twelve now and still waiting for Nat's chair. It faced
away from *Jesus in Agony in the Garden*. The five-by-seven-foot
painting, an incandescence of red and purple framed in brilliant
gold leaf, overwhelmed the small dining room like prayers
blaring over a loudspeaker. But it was the eyes that bothered
Molly. They were big and doleful, pleading toward heaven. Con-
sidering *Jesus's* dilemma, her worry over the piano seemed inap-
propriate and even rude. She was trying mightily *not* to think
about the piano.

"Where in hell's it gonna fit?" That was Nat. He sat down in
front of the painting and plunked his book on the table, fluttering the pages like bird wings until he found his place.

She shrugged hard, wishing they'd hear him when he cursed.
Just once. The caned seat of her chair creaked as she shifted.
Already she was loaded down with *when* and here he was piling
on *where*. *When* was soon, *where* she didn't know. Under the
tablecloth she played "Tarantella" on her knees with both hands
and was altogether unsettled. Cautiously, she looked up. Just as
before—time and again, Jesus was doubled on the wall. Two

brilliant gold leaf frames. Two incandescent purple robes; two red mantles; and knotted in prayer, two pairs of pale hands resting on two gray boulders. Pleading toward heaven were the four big doleful eyes.

Sometimes she'd stare into the mirror to see if one of her own eyes was more deeply brown than the other, or more almond in shape, some sign that would explain her peculiar vision. Always in the mirror Molly's eyes *looked* normal, but her ways of seeing were something like the work of a bumbling photographer: either two prints of the same negative, such as the Jesuses on the wall, or a haze of two *different* things at once, like the double exposure that pictured her Godmother Byrd standing shoulder-to-shoulder with Grandmother Willie when, in truth, they'd not even seen each other since the wedding of Molly's parents more than two decades ago. If Byrd and Willie saw themselves in the same photograph, they'd both have a fit.

Byrd Maclaurin was a Catholic; Willie Haxton Hardy, a Baptist. Like pouring holy water into a font, Byrd, the dutiful godmother, filled Molly with the great drama and mystery of Catholicism; Grandmother Willie worked prodigiously to save her from that same Roman Church, a thing so bedeviled and foreign it was governed by an Italian posing as Christ on earth. She imagined the Jesuses refereeing as Byrd and Willie pulled her side from side in a religious tug-of-war, her eyeballs bursting—*pop, pop*—just as they split her down the middle. She squeezed her eyelids shut, waited a tight second or two, then peered at the painting through the squint, forcing the left eye to fall in with the right. One Jesus.

Her father, Jim Flanagan, had said that the painting once hung in a flophouse on Mulberry Street owned by his father. Molly wondered why he'd seemed so proud, and then why the pawky smile had slid off his face so quickly.

He had refused to consider her mother's suggestion—made in a voice so high Molly was sure she'd rehearsed it—that the painting might well be appreciated over at the Monastery of the Poor Clares. "And deprive Willie?" He had screwed up his face, then laughed. "Certainly not. She'd lose her grip." Grandmother Willie had said that Jesus would never have worn such wild colors—that the painting was very nearly immodest. She hadn't seemed at all surprised that it had belonged to *his* family.

At least he hadn't enshrined Saint Cuthbert in the dining room, though Molly knew he'd considered it. Instead, that painting hung in the living room over the fireplace above the mantle. The legend was that the saint had spent long nocturnal hours praying while standing up to his armpits in the angry Irish Sea. When at last he'd come out of the cold water, two otters had dried his feet with their fur, then licked them warm with their pink tongues. In truth, the otters in the painting bared their teeth like a pair of mean brown dogs intent on biting the white ankles of Saint Cuthbert the way they might the postman's.

Her father came into the dining room and sat down. He quickly said the blessing, the syllables of prayer toppling into one long word that sounded neither English or Latin. He finished before she blinked. "Have at it," he said, reaching for the newspaper as he crossed himself. Catholics said the same shapeless prayer over and over again, even when certain dinners such as fried chicken or barbecue deserved greater thanks. Protestants invented new ways of saying grace over each and every meal no matter what was served. Even so, she hated eating with the Protestant cousins, because sometimes they'd call on her to say grace. She'd sit there not knowing whether to go on and make the Sign of the Cross—when she did they'd stare like she was about to issue an incantation—or just keep her hands in her lap and mumble the same old "Bless Us, O Lord."

Nat always said the blessing as if each meal were the Last Supper, but his slow-moving reverence had kept their father from the morning paper once too often. Now Nat was allowed to give thanks only for dinner. Molly was no longer asked to take a turn at all. She had persisted rather stubbornly in substituting Holy Ghost for God or Jesus. She would say, "Bless us, O Holy Ghost, and these thy gifts." She felt God and Jesus got more attention than They deserved, so she directed all prayers solely to the Holy Ghost, hoping in some small way to make up for the years, even centuries, of neglect. In return, the Holy Ghost had rid her room of the snakes after God and Jesus had failed her. And now, convinced that the Holy Ghost was responsible for sending the piano, she was grateful—mightily grateful—and silently prayed that He'd hurry it up.

She stuck her spoon into the bowl of purplish oatmeal. A burst of heat shot up, hazing her glasses. Across from her, Nat appeared as the faint silhouette of a man lost in a snowstorm. But she couldn't imagine him getting lost—getting his way, more likely. She cleared her glasses with the napkin as the oatmeal vapor drifted past Nat and on toward the painting where it clung as morning fog in the Garden of Gethsemane. Nat was fifteen and had sat with his back to the big, miserable Jesus longer than was fair, but she was not going to ask for his chair until her birthday, when no one, not even Nat, could object.

"Ike's king of the cold war," said her father from behind the wall of *Commercial Appeal*. He folded the paper and propped it against the milk bottle, sniffing slightly as if the news held an odor. She knew he was talking about bombs.

Her cheeks puffed with the heat as she took a bite.

"It's cooler just around the rim, angel."

Getting the oatmeal down his way—a ritual of tiny bites spooned clockwise from around the bowl—would take all morning and she wanted to finish before the piano was delivered. The anticipation was building as a crescendo. Music was the sound of time and it was playing in her head. "On Wings of Song . . ."

"Have some cream, angel." Without looking up, he slid the pitcher toward her, its cobalt blue the only color that stood up against the reflected purple of the painting. Absorbed as he was with the morning paper, he never had noticed that she didn't use cream. Breakfast meant oatmeal. Disguising it wouldn't change anything.

Nat flipped the page of his book that he held like a steering wheel, his shoulders vibrating as if he were in a car on a bumpy road as he laughed silently inside himself. The table shook.

"*Penrod*?" asked her father, his nose still buried in the quivering newspaper, and Nat nodded that it was. Her father looked up with dancing blue eyes. His fingers were gray with newsprint as he turned to the financial section. "Into the tar yet?" He sounded hopeful, as if Nat were on the brink of an important discovery and should hurry.

"That was last chapter," smiled Nat, still reading as he talked. His bright hazel eyes seemed to change colors as they rolled across the pages—amber, then green—traveling easily, even joyfully, through the story. The truth was that among dozens of other books, he'd read the tattered *Penrod* five or six times, always laughing hard as though each chapter held surprises. As a boy, her father had also read this book, and he and Nat now shared the episodes, recalling each incident as if they themselves had actually lived it at the exact same time. Penrod and Sam.

In the way that one might long to know a family secret, she too wanted to read *Penrod*, but she felt that they would not want her in on it, and had yet to take the book from the shelf.

The Flanagans never talked much at breakfast. Her mother rarely even sat down to it, moving instead about the kitchen, making the soft sounds of morning: opening the window, swishing water in the sink, stirring the oatmeal, the sounds all linked by the bronchial wheeze in her chest that was chronically persistent.

Coming from the kitchen, Elizabeth Flanagan paused in the doorway as if she might knock before entering the dining room. Molly watched her mother's olive skin blanch as she struggled with the painting, the delirium of color something she'd known little of when dressed in the brown of her Protestant upbringing.

Elizabeth Hardy Flanagan had converted to Catholic, yet never seemed wholly that. The Hardys were a mix of Methodist and Baptist and Evangelical, all bound together in a bundle of plainness and austerity. Jim Flanagan said they'd "sprung up from the bowels of Mississippi, so forgive them for not appreciating the drama and color of a good ceremony."

Whenever he poked fun at her family, she held her lips tight together, yet by her silence seemed to agree with him. Judas Iscariot, Molly thought.

"It won't be for long now," her mother said, speaking of the piano and letting one of her country idioms slip out before she could catch it. Her hair was brushed back from her face and she was pretty with only the faint touch of lipstick. She wore an apron of blue forget-me-nots, as she stood in the doorway between two worlds.

The Flanagans' small Cape Cod house, stuffed as it was with Victorian trappings, appeared as a dollhouse furnished with real people's furniture. And now the piano. Molly decided not to ask *where* it would fit, afraid they'd change their minds. She knew her father would not part with any of his possessions.

She guessed that he'd kept all these things out of loyalty to the dead: his parents, Nate and Clare Flanagan; his grandmother, Mama Jo Culligan. Each one had died just after the next, like the felling of a grove of old oaks.

Their treasures included the red velvet settee and matching chair with each arm curled in what seemed a one-way journey to the center of the earth, the green leather lounge chair that inclined almost to the sleeping position, and the Ansonia clock guarded by wild-eyed twin griffins that looked menacing and suspiciously ill-suited for the job. The chairs and settee always seemed occupied by the ghosts of the Flanagan family. They crowded the house that was already barely big enough for the living. Molly imagined stacking the ghosts on top of one another in order to make way for the piano. She pictured them standing on her father's shoulders like a family of circus performers.

Then she imagined the Flanagan ghosts all straddling one end of a seesaw, their weightless spirits held down by their living stand-in, her Godmother Byrd. All of them were balanced against the weight of Grandmother Willie, alone on the other end and holding steady.

Molly reached for the milk bottle, and her father instinctively secured his paper with both hands. She poured milk in the glass embossed with the map of Florida, remembering too late — around Apalachicola — that it was meant for the orange juice. She filled it to Tallahassee anyhow. Nat, already finished, placed his napkin on the table and stood up. He wore a black T-shirt and as he picked the toast point from his plate, eating it ceremoniously as if it were the Holy Eucharist, he looked like a young priest. She smiled to herself, imagining the fire in Grandmother Willie's face if such a thing should ever happen.

"What time's the piano coming?" He rocked back and forth as though the piano were already there and someone had begun to play a tune. "My Babe," or something.

She shrugged at the mention of the piano as if it were a toy she'd outgrown. Waiting for the piano was like wishing for snow in Memphis; you could count on it only after it hit the ground. When snow did come, stilling the world with a quiet as sparkling as a newborn star, you could then feel hope rising inside, the long wait dead and buried under the blanket of white.

But she would not say this—or anything else—to Nat. She had yet to forgive him for Sunday, when he contorted his features, dragging his leg and lunging after her all the way home from Little Flower Church. She'd been breathless, afraid, with him dogging after her drooling real spit. She'd reached the house just inches ahead of him, charged up the steps, flung open the door, and had seen—there on the footstool in the living room—*The Hunchback of Notre Dame.* "Legerdemain, angel," her father had said, patting her on the back in consolation and all the while shaking his head. "Look it up and try to remember next time." That Nat had once again tricked her into playing a leading role in one of his dramas still stung. As she looked at him now, she saw the vague semblance of that same grotesquery, awaiting only the slightest inspiration to again transform his otherwise handsome face.

Quasimodo was only one of the identities Nat had assumed. He had been, all in the month of August, Mr. Dick, blind Pew— "an exceptional Pew," her father had said—and Friar Tuck. Grandmother Willie vehemently disapproved of his performances. She would shake her head, saying that Nat should give up fiction and spend more time with King James. But her exhortations bounced off Nat like arrows hitting a shield. Molly wondered why it was that his hide was ten times thicker than her own.

Nat's eyes sawed back and forth between Molly and the orange-juice glass. "Oh, I get it," he said, as though struck suddenly by a remarkable revelation. "White's for sand. Very clever."

She felt a burning in her throat. Over the Atlantic Ocean just east of St. Augustine the sun was white as it would never be again. She looked away from him and quickly drank the milk, tasting her own irritation.

"Golly, Molly, what time's the concerto?" he wheedled. "'The Volga Boatman.' You got that one down great!" He started singing in a low-down voice. "Aye-yookh-nyem! Aye-yookh-nyem! We are toil . . . oil . . . oil . . . ing!" He swayed back and forth, and suddenly she knew that in the months to come, she must find a way to keep him from coming to her recital. Her progress in the John Thompson series had been slow. She could see by the bookmark in *Penrod* that he'd read fifteen or so pages as he downed his oatmeal doused with cream, the milk, several pieces of toast slathered with marmalade, and the orange juice drunk from a Florida glass—all of it accomplished without so much as dropping a crumb. And his straight, dark brown hair never seemed to need combing. She stiffened her resolve not to speak to him. She pictured his face turned ugly with worry, his concentration waylaid, his hearty laughter reduced to a shiver. That's how it would be *after* her birthday when she'd sit in his chair and read *Penrod: His Complete Story.*

She felt the same as when she had admired the bracelet of tiny silver roses in her Godmother Byrd's jewelry box, hoping to receive it for Christmas. All she'd done then was hold the bracelet up to the light, but when Byrd handed her the box on

Christmas Eve she guessed what was inside and felt a little sly. She'd worn it the following Saturday to her music lesson at Willie's. Seated beside her at the old upright piano, Grandmother Willie had looked down at the bracelet and said "*Spanish*," in a voice so cold it seemed to tarnish one of the roses. Then Molly had made more mistakes than usual that day and Willie would only say, "Begin again. From the beginning."

Sometimes she practiced at Byrd's. Seated at the baby grand, Molly would watch the reflection of her own fingers in the lacquered sheen that mirrored the keyboard as she played "On Wings of Song," "Minuet in G," or "Londonderry Air"—only vaguely aware of the keys bumping into and tripping over the dreams of performing on stage that floated through her head. Always Byrd listened from the far corner of the front porch.

As soon as Molly finished practicing, Byrd would switch on the phonograph, playing the recordings that she loved—"The Harmonious Blacksmith" or "Ride of the Valkyries" or "Rosamunde." More often it was the "Ave Maria." Byrd would insist that Molly listen closely because the aria was "alive with the spirit of Clare and Mama Jo." Hearing it, Molly would feel the ancestral circle slowly close around her—against the evangelism of Grandmother Willie—but it lasted only so long as the music played.

More often Molly practiced on Mrs. Flynn's old out-of-tune upright, but only an hour a week, since her mother didn't like being obligated to the next-door neighbors. While Molly played, the Widow Flynn and her spinster sister, Miss Anna Doyle, would rock in time to their own knit-one, purl-twos—always in a counter rhythm to Molly's selection and at a faster tempo. Her father had asked, did she "appreciate the intrepid spirit of her audience?" Until then she had pretended her mistakes were few, ignoring Byrd's consistent choice of a seat in the distant outpost of the porch as well as the sisters' swags of gray hair fat as muffs over their cotton-stuffed ears. Having her own piano, she thought, would fix things.

"So what time?" Nat still wanted an answer to the piano question when they heard the sound of smashing glass from across the street. The Finches throwing things at each other was nothing new, but lately the fights occurred more frequently.

"Round one," said Nat. He was shadowboxing and hit the paper.

Her father smiled a crooked smile, but refused to look up. "Longest fight in history. Ref, ring the bell." He turned to the editorial page, his eyes settling on the cartoon.

Elizabeth Flanagan shook her head. "Just hope it's over and done before Mother gets here."

Molly coughed hard. She hadn't counted on seeing Grandmother Willie today. The music in her head slowed to a dirge. Every Saturday morning Molly rode the bus to Willie's house, where she was taught to play the piano; afterwards she would often spend the night with Byrd. For each encounter with Willie her father insisted on an interlude with her godmother. The rhythms were different, the themes oddly the same.

For Byrd, music was the art of angels, the sounds of it pouring from the phonograph inspired prayer and lifted her one step closer to heaven. Grandmother Willie pounded out hymns, the craft of piano playing—*Praise the Lord*—a sure-fire way to salvation. Without knowing it, Grandmother Willie and God-mother Byrd were point and counterpoint. Willie was tudda *rum* tudda *rum* tudda *rum*; Byrd was rum *tudda*.

On this Saturday Molly had thought she was receiving a reprieve along with the second-hand piano, but now Grand-mother Willie Haxton Hardy herself would show up just in time to spoil things. She felt the relentless ticking of Willie's metronome.

Nat tried again. "Dad, what if Mr. Finch killed Mrs. Finch? With a butcher knife. Or an ax." Her father, absorbed with the line-up for the World Series, waved him out of the room. Nat hummed his sort of departing tune as he left the table. "Take me out to the ball game . . . take me out to the crowd." He was not good at baseball. Molly was glad of it.

"Put on some music, Nat," said her father. "Something lively."

Her father rustled his paper as he turned from sports to comics. Molly was halfway through the oatmeal when Massenet's "Élégie" came from the phonograph. An expression of sadness slid across her father's face. "Not that, Mr. Micawber," he called. "*Il Trovatore*." He would listen to the whole opera just to hear "The Anvil Chorus." Then the clock gonged from the living room. The deep tone always seemed to come from far away.

SOMETIMES AT night she denied the sound of the clock, the heaviness of sleep staving off the advancing hour, the hollows of her mind then filling with dreams. In them she was often chased by something she never could see and she woke with sweaty pajamas sticking to her skin. Then too, there were nights when she could not escape from a huge stone house with hundreds of rooms or from a labyrinth of streets lined with ominous gray ramshackle buildings, until she heard the gong of the clock and, just before awakening, pictured the two griffins clinging to the sides of it, their mouths open as though they would consume the hour. And she knew that some night she'd again be that same small dot on a plain where she had felt, time and again, the vastness of space lying beyond, a vision of eternity. She had kept these old dreams in memory. They were the whisperings of the Holy Ghost.

"Achooie! Achoo-ie! Achooie!" The painting rattled against the wall. Her father sneezed loud enough to register on the Richter scale. Everything done heartily—that was her father. She looked to see if he'd blown a hole in the paper. "Turn up the music, Nat," he called.

LATELY, WHENEVER the clock gonged in the night, time prickled her ears and she would wake remembering the snakes she had seen years before, and although she no longer saw them, she still remembered the awful fear pounding in her chest.

At the time, her father, pretending to believe her, had offered to "stab the apparitions" with the umbrella, but her mother had bristled up and said he was catering to a childish imagination. Elizabeth Flanagan was unable to recognize the genus *Desperatus*; for her, apparitions were no different than books of fiction, fabricated things that were the same as lies. She thought loose fibers of the mind needed a tight weave of moderation and strength of purpose to overcome reckless import. Had she known, Willie would have said the same thing. Back then—at the age of six, surrounded by snakes and holding no powers of persuasion—Molly had cut holes in her new pajamas, afterwards blaming the snakes and hoping her mother would believe they existed.

One night, Molly stood in the hall calling her father, having bravely stepped over a bright green garden snake near the side of the bed, and he came into her room, quietly pretending that he was St. Patrick. After he directed her to step back over the green snake, back into the bed, he made the Sign of the Cross with a flourish, commanding the snakes "Begone" in a voice louder than he intended. He quickly shushed himself, put his finger to his lips, and then stood perfectly still and quiet with his hands folded in prayer. She'd guessed that her father wasn't altogether holy when, after the attempted exorcism, the snakes had multiplied. At least the two new anacondas on the bottom bookcase were smaller than the old fat ones that had coiled on top.

There was one reassuring thing about the snakes: they had not moved. They had not crawled or shown initiative. Each night they appeared in the same place as before—the king snake wound tightly around a rung on her rocking chair like thread on a spool, the blue garters stretched along the ceiling the same as molding, and the python—silver and black with red eyes—corkscrewed over and under Burgess, Twain, Malory, and the row of Sabatinis on the bookshelf.

The reason the snakes had lived for so long a time in her room was that she'd wasted weeks by asking *God* to kill them. When they persisted in appearing night after night, she had turned to Jesus, but without results. Finally, after pleading with the Holy Ghost in a silent prayer of desperation, the snakes had vacated her room. Faith was a tongue of fire.

Now, she waited, recalling the gongs of a few moments ago— three, four, or was it five . . . knowing that the clock would lag ever more slowly with each passing hour and would soon stop altogether. The piano would come after that. She unwrapped her feet from the chair legs and pressed her right foot to the floor as if to a pedal. At the same time, the house swelled with the hammer of the smithy and the chorus of voices.

"It's eight-fifteen, Jim." Her mother begged just as she did every Saturday morning. She wanted him to wind and set the clock, a thing he had never done and would never do, until Sunday night. The clock had belonged to *his* father and somehow, the ritual did, too.

"Predictable," mumbled her father, skipping the obituaries and going on to real estate.

After the clock stopped its tick-tocking and the hourly and half-hourly strikes, Saturdays seemed to last longer; the rattle and hum of the Flanagan household set the pattern and rhythm of the day instead. Still, Molly wondered why her father seemed to refuse, time and again, to accept her mother's suggestion that it was only a sixth-day clock.

Her mother poured him a third cup of coffee and the first one for herself. He was humming along with the chorus and reading at the same time. He preferred the dimmer light, but she raised the shade anyhow, flooding the room with sun. Suddenly everything turned pastel. "I saw the light," he said, mocking her. His sandy red hair flecked with gray looked like tarnished silver in the intense light. He squinted at the paper as if the yellow news hurt his eyes. Not really wanting to talk, he offered her a section. "Getcha paper right here. Read all about it."

"No, thanks." Molly's mother was only interested in the baby now. Although it never seemed so, she was much younger than Molly's father, but still older than most expectant mothers. Molly was not supposed to know about the baby yet, just as she wasn't supposed to know about most things, but sometimes at dawn their quiet talk became a boat floating through her head, carrying their secrets.

From the spoon shaking a little in her mother's hand, sugar sifted into her cup like falling snow. Molly looked at her mother's face and for a moment studied the uneasiness there. She wondered if Grandmother Willie knew about the baby— another Catholic grandchild in the making. And she felt a slight chill.

For Willie, Catholics were the black sheep of mankind. Most likely she'd try lulling the baby with hymns and then luring it to the Baptist Church in the same way she'd done Molly. Once, when she'd been tempted to accept the invitation, she had felt the black shadow of mortal sin touch her from behind before she regained her senses and escaped it by an inch. Willie might well be the Devil disguised in a housedress.

"Molly, pull your eyes together," said her mother.

She squeezed her eyes to slits and focused within the squint. The shade flapped on the roller in the living room. Nat had lowered it and then let go. Determined that he would not get the first look at the piano, Molly swallowed the last bite of oatmeal and hastily excused herself.

ON THE petit-point pillow that rested on the settee, the wings of a moth fluttered in two-four time. Nat hovered in front of the window, the reflection of his eyes like an owl's. Molly stood in the doorway adjusting her own eyes to the darkened room. The walls were dappled with the shadows of two huge elms—*Ulmus americana* her father always said—that stood in the front yard. Her father's talk embraced a modicum of Latin phrases, but she thought his name for the elms was a kind of patriotism, the same as his spirited reminders that her birth in 1943 was a major event between Pearl Harbor and Hiroshima, and that she should not forget it. Her mother disagreed—she did not think Molly should equate life with disaster. But they *had* built their house on land her father had inherited from his father. Grandmother Willie said that the lot was shady in more ways than one and that living on ground once owned by Nate Flanagan was disaster *in and of itself*.

Built years later than the other houses on Theola Avenue, the Flanagans' was one of a kind and didn't seem to belong there. The yard was once a tennis court and some of the old people in the neighborhood—Mrs. Flynn and Mr. Remmler, for instance—still referred to it as "Flanagan's Court." Molly closed her eyes and imagined the house gone . . . and then herself facing Grandfather Nate on the opposite side of the net, the grit surface beneath their feet. He listed a little to the left, then whacked the ball to her forehand with his cane. Molly had trouble with balls of any sort, since one of her eyes always strayed off on its own and was unreliable when it came time to hit or catch one, but she swung hard with the heavy racket strung with catgut—she thought it was cruel about the cat— and missed, the ball sailing over her head and landing in the bayou where it floated like a white lily in the brown water.

"What's with the arm swinging?" asked Nat. "Dad, please own up that Molly was adopted."

She opened her eyes. Nat was looking at her, smirking and shaking his head, then he turned back to the window. Pictures of all the ancestors sat on the table. Their faces looked out at her from the distance of time: the round figure of Mama Jo in a long black dress; Grandmother Clare, pretty in lace with her hair knotted thickly on top of her head; and Grandfather Nate in an overcoat and with a scarf thrown casually over his shoulder. They appeared to have lived in three different climates. She hadn't known them, but sometimes they seemed as real to her as the living. She might learn "Clair de Lune." In honor of the ghosts, she would play it for Byrd, who had been their friend. She knew better than to play it for Willie.

Nat moved slightly as she came toward the window, allowing her space enough to watch. He was humming "The Volga Boatman." Molly looked up and down the street. No sign of the van. Through a gap in the thick green bowers of oaks, the sun shone on the Finches' yard like a spotlight. Mrs. Finch was stumbling up the front steps and almost fell. Mr. Finch got in the car, slammed the door and just sat there, his hands clenched on the steering wheel like a man in heavy traffic. Their four children stood on the porch—fifteen-year-old Ray, his thin pompadour slick with brilliantine; Jane, fourteen and amazingly pretty; and the barefoot towheads, four-year-old Sue and Jimmy, seven. All of them either straddled the porch rails or held onto the square posts, looking as afraid and miserable as a wagonload of migrants.

"It was a draw," said Nat. "She missed him by a mile." Molly laughed, then wished she hadn't. She was watching Jane and, even from the distance, read the face full of hurt. Jane's fingers combed through her long brown hair as if untangling the mess of worries. Then she drew the silken strands to one side and loosely wove a plait that hung over her shoulder. She pulled a red ribbon from her pocket and tied the end. Jane's brother, Ray, was staring at her. Suddenly he reached over, grabbed the plait, and jerked hard, hitting her head on the porch post, but she didn't call out. She backed away from him, then ran down the steps, holding her head. And suddenly a faceless warning came to Molly out of nowhere—"Iceman!" Then it was gone. She shuddered for Jane.

Molly saw Nat's jaw stiffen in the glass before it clouded with his breath. He said nothing, the words held inside the prison of his clenched teeth. In the Flanagan family things never boiled over, they just rolled and bubbled under a lid clamped down tight, the puffs of escaping steam thin and disappearing.

"Pull down the shade, Nat," said their mother from the dining room. "Watching, you're no better than they are."

Nat stalled in the same way he refused to close a book until he finished the chapter. He fumbled with the cord as the sun slanted through the window sidelong and warm as desire, something like the way he was looking at Jane. His eyes were deep green and glimmering with her movement. Jane had joined hands with Sue and Jimmy and was whirling round and round with them, laughing. She was laughing at Ray. He turned and glowered at her before going inside, slamming the door behind him.

Nat was rigid. "Goddamn mean son of a bitch. He's mad as hell because she didn't cry."

At that moment Molly recognized something powerful in her brother, a surging strength of feeling as mysterious as any growing thing. Jane looked toward the Flanagans' house as if she felt his eyes. She was tall and slim, flipping her head like a nervous horse shaking its mane.

Sliding onto his long, slender finger, the ring of the pull-cord was silky, almost white; he turned it round and round until the cord twisted into a rope. When he released it the ring bounced and twirled like a ballerina. *Il Trovatore* was over and a new record had begun. Molly was hearing the overture. She could not think the name—then it came to her—"Rosamunde." He pulled the shade down only after Jane had danced up the front steps and gone inside. The lump of silence Nat swallowed seemed to bob mercilessly in his throat. Then he left the room.

Elizabeth Flanagan looked in to make sure the shade was down, then turned back to the kitchen. "Common," she said unequivocally, as if stating a mathematical fact. Elizabeth

Flanagan was indignant whenever the Finches brought their fights out in the open. She didn't believe in doing much of anything in the front yard and even faulted Old Man Remmler two houses down for planting the rainbow of biennials out front last June—"At least he could have chosen just one color instead of planting a box of crayons."

Molly considered the cluster of hollyhocks Mr. Remmler's family, each one six-foot tall, like him, and friendly as sunshine. She quietly raised the shade and looked down the street toward his yard. The big flowers were prideful and strong as trees. Over at the Finches' a pigeon cooed beneath the round attic window that looked like a glass eye. Not so much as a clump of clover or a sprig of grass grew in the shadow of the tall house. The barren, dusty yard was patterned with footprints that seemed somehow the markings of primitive man before talk got started. She thought that if the Finches planted hollyhocks, hibiscus, maybe even zinnias or iris, white and yellow and purple iris, even *brown* iris—that something good might happen there.

From the back of the house, her father was singing "Londonderry Air," holding each low note with a booming affection. When his breath ran out, he whistled the high notes in falsetto, which seemed to stir the huddle of ghosts. A cane thumped. A throat cleared. Then the scent of a perfume unlike her mother's Tigress or Essence de Chantilly filled the room. Molly held her breath against the sweetness.

The strips of light through the louvered door appeared like bars on a page of sheet music and she thought how her father's voice would soon sound more rich and lustrous when she accompanied him on her own piano. She imagined the ghosts joining in, a silent chorus, their dark lips moving out of tempo in varied ranges that only spirits could hear—the unearthly baritone of Nate Flanagan and the lilting sopranos of Clare and Mama Jo. She opened the door and stepped out on the stoop to wait.

Chapter TWO

Molly blinked to focus. A block away Lena was standing with Essie on that same-as-everyday square of sidewalk reserved, it seemed, for finishing their conversations. Essie's hands suggested sound as she waved them like a conductor. The black polka dots on her dress became hundreds of quarter notes bouncing in rhythm. Essie Stout worked for Molly's cousins, the Mahons, across the street; Lena Mills, for the Flanagans. Lena stood tall and patient, confined to Essie's talk. Molly hadn't told Lena about the piano, wanting to surprise her. Had Lena known, she wouldn't have stood there listening to Essie.

Lena lived in Klondike, which was the colored neighborhood, and though it was close by, it might well have been as far away as Alaska. In the backyard, when she was small, Molly would look across the bayou toward Klondike—the bayou had seemed as wide as a mile—and clearly see the black people rolling along the sidewalk on Jackson Avenue, going into and out of Mr. Tarantino's store, talking, eating cake. Gradually the chinaberry trees her mother had planted fenced them from sight, along with the thick tangle of wild thorny rose vines that had grown up soon after.

Molly sat on the ground, feeling the warm earth. With a stick she began forming a river in the dust and beside it mapped out a city. Between streets she dug bayous and built bridges, the building of the bridges being the most interesting part. Along the river she formed Indian mounds, capping the lumps of dirt with carpets of soldier's moss. She filled her mother's watering can and flooded the river and the bayous. Then she drew a square park and inside the perimeter, built an octagonal bandstand from twigs. She imagined herself playing the piano there—songs she didn't yet know, like "Musette" and "Sonatina"—forgetting the great difficulty she'd experienced in building even her very limited repertoire of primary tunes.

From the other side of the narrow street Little Alfred, her five-year-old cousin interrupted, calling her name over and over again. He sat crosslegged on the curb holding a long stick in his hand as if fishing in the street. With his short muscular legs and thick blond hair that curled in the heat, he looked like a small version of the famous wrestler, Gorgeous George. "Come on over," he kept yelling. He was stuck, like her father's "Toreador" record when it got to the part where Ezio Pinza loudly sang "O . . . O . . . O . . ." never getting the whole of it out. A wearisome thing. But in spite of the sound of his voice, her attention, riveted as it was on the "Musette" still playing in her head, was inviolate.

"You can play with Bud," he said, persisting.

It wasn't true. His old black and white fox terrier, Bud, wouldn't allow a pat from anyone but him. Bud sat there beside him, dribbling spit and wagging his tail, a false friendliness she had come to recognize. Once, when she'd walked across the Mahons' porch and surprised him as he slept beside the front door, he woke and nipped her, appearing then as a two-headed dog. Right now he was only a dog-and-a-half.

"I've got marbles," said Alfred, selecting a blue and green jumbo from his pocket and holding it up above his head, like a small magician attempting to mesmerize her with chubby sleight-of-hand. She looked up and for an instant saw the one big marble as two—both of them, no matter how intensely blue-green and sparkling, just variations of his theme. She hummed "Musette" and kept working in the dirt.

Then he pretended to clear his throat and said, "The river's going to flood."

She'd worried that rain might prevent the delivery and now pictured herself seated before the wet keyboard of a piano that was top-heavy and swaying in the floodwater, playing "Blow the Man Down." That was the song her father always sang—*loud* when he shaved or showered, *louder* when he gargled.

"What about a flood, Alfred?" Molly hadn't spoken all morning and hardly recognized her own voice. She'd used the high-toned voice of Charlotte, her neighbor down the street. She truly hated Charlotte's way of talking, bossy and out of sorts, and now she regretted saying anything at all.

"It's going to rain and never stop," said Alfred, matter-of-factly.

Alfred had no Protestant affiliations. She doubted that he had even heard of the Bible. "Forty days and nights?" she asked, knowing he wouldn't have any idea.

"Five," he said with certainty. He became a scribe, scratching in the street with his stick. In truth he didn't yet know how to read or write. But the way he'd learned everything else so quickly, Molly knew it wouldn't be long.

"We could make a canoe out of branches," he said. "Then we'd be saved."

She looked over and saw his face clouded like the sky. He hadn't yet learned to swim, either. "You're not going to drown," she said. She thought of telling him the story about Noah just to shut him up, but she didn't really want to think about the Bible today. Already she worried that Willie had so filled her full of the Bible stories that she might turn into a *Baptist*. On the other hand, Godmother Byrd held her spellbound with stories about purity, which is what nuns were all about. Molly didn't want to be a *nun* anymore than she wanted to be a *Baptist*. All she wanted was to play the piano and fly with the Holy Ghost.

Alfred called her again. Ignoring him was impossible, so she gave up and said, "Why don't you ask if you can come over here?" She didn't really want his company, but it was better than going over there and chancing a dog bite. "Not Bud," she added.

He jumped up and ran into his house. She was mad at herself for letting him distract her from thinking "Musette." Now the music playing in her head was a watery *H.M.S. Pinafore*.

Out of the house like a flash flood, he stood on the curb, waiting. "You have to watch me cross." He was frowning, obviously disgruntled with the limits of his own age. His mother, Frances, was going to have a baby. She was about five months along. Molly thought that Alfred would feel better when he was no longer an only child.

Bud beat his tail on the sidewalk and barked, all of it in three-quarter time. Alfred pointed a finger and reluctantly told him to stay. Bud didn't like being left behind, but sat still because Alfred was king. Bud cocked his head like Nipper on the RCA Victor records.

Alfred came over and when Molly gave him his own territory, he settled into his work with a diligence that surprised her. He mapped out a small farm, unusual since she was sure he had never seen one. Her own Grandaddy Bob raised cows down at Horn Lake, so at the age of eleven and a half Molly had seen quite a lot of farm life. Her mother said *she* had seen as much of it as she wanted, and didn't want to see more. Molly thought it was mean-spirited to hate where you came from.

Alfred was humming "Dixie."

"This yard was once a tennis court," she said, giving Alfred the history of his land, but omitting the part about the underworld connection. "That's why it's hard to make the river flow just right. The land's too flat."

"Oh, that's all right," he said, looking up. His eyes were pools of bright blue. "Farms are supposed to be. Mine's growing cotton. They call it white gold unless the boll weevils get in it. Then I don't know what they call it."

Alfred was clearly a genius and she hoped the new cousin would be as smart. Molly hadn't thought much about her own mother's baby since it was probably only about one month along. Changes did not easily assemble in her mind, but just then she wondered how her family would fit five people around the square table.

Her left eye caught sight of a dead locust, yellow as an old man's fingernail. She picked the shell off the bark of the elm and handed it to Alfred who collected such things. He stuck it on the pocket flap of his shirt where he could admire it at a glance. She considered telling him the story of the locust plague in the Bible, but he interrupted her with "*ta dan*," the first two notes of "Hungarian Rhapsody." Bud wagged his tail like a baton and barked flatly. Suddenly, from down the sidewalk came Lena, waving her arms and shouting—her sound close to C-sharp, the octave above middle C.

Pete, Mr. Remmler's pet goose, was flapping his wings and pecking her heels in staccato. Lena ran fast, her thin legs testing her strength and then some. Essie was on the other side of the street now and heading for the Mahons'. She yelled for help, but was not about to enter the fracas herself. Alfred and Molly both jumped up and ran toward Lena, almost running her down. Then Pete, not so feisty and mean with three against him, ran for his life, for Lena had turned around and gotten after him with her black purse that was big as a satchel. Pete was speedy for a fat, waddling bird, and gained momentum enough to propel himself over Mr. Remmler's fence, into the safety of the backyard.

"The Lord's done sent me a sign," declared Lena. She was mad and out of breath. She fanned herself with the broadbrim straw hat banded with orange and red ribbons. "I'm seeing it clear."

"Amen," said Essie from across the street. A red carnation pinned up high on her shoulder looked like a bird.

"*What* do you see?" Alfred was ready for the enlightenment. "Jesus, or what?"

"I'm seeing Pete in a pot!" Lena held her arms up to the sky like a gospel singer, this vision of revenge spreading over her face in a bitter sweet glow. Molly pictured Pete plucked of feathers and laid out in the black enameled pan, high-sided like a coffin, a funeral spray of parsley garnishing his long neck and head.

She watched Lena out of one eye and Mr. Remmler out of the other. Just under the surface she felt the stark tension of contrast between black and white, and the threat of words yet unspoken. She'd felt it time and again, ever since she could remember. Mr. Remmler ambled toward them, looking not at all apologetic. Lena planted her feet firmly in place.

"Just look a there, woman," he said, pointing to the evidence, a trail of feathers enough for a Chickasaw chief's bonnet. "You 'bout ran all the meat off his bones." But Mr. Remmler fussed without conviction. He had used up most of his energy just walking over to complain and now his voice faded to a whisper.

And Lena was not afraid of an old white man anyhow. She raised her shoulders like a sleek black cat's. "You just lucky his big web-feet paddled hisself on home. I'd of wrung his big gobbler neck on the spot if I'd caught up with him, I'm telling." She huffed at him with stinging breath. She ate peculiar food, carp and rutabagas.

He wore an argyle sweater. In the flat, warm air, he smelled sour. As the threat of ugly words receded back underground, Molly managed to focus her eyes in spite of his odor, which, merged with Lena's, was now overpowering.

"Fate was on the bird's side, I guess." He'd said all he had to say and he began to back away. He stopped just long enough to stoop and pick up a feather that he stuck in Alfred's thick yellow thatch of hair like a royal plume. The old man followed the trail of feathers, bending and gathering them like wild flowers before wobbling up his porch steps.

In early summer Molly's mother had gotten on Mr. Remmler about keeping poultry in town more than a decade after the war effort was over. "Likely it's his feed keeping up those filthy pigeons." More than once she had told Molly's father, that "some people"—meaning Mr. Remmler—"just don't know when to end a thing. The need for a Victory Garden is long gone and he's still farming in the city." Her mother exaggerated, but Mr. Remmler did grow pole beans in summer in the little space alongside his house where most people raised privet hedges. By July, the bean vines would grow thickly over the poles, making beautiful green teepees, and he would allow Molly to go in one, but only after she promised to be careful and not disturb the beans.

"You still be playing in the dirt and all," Lena saw. "Those big gals ain't going to have no associating with you." Molly knew that when Lena found out about the piano she'd think otherwise. Charlotte and Jane would be busting to see it.

But Molly wasn't paying close attention to her, thinking instead how Mr. Remmler loved animals and would never have cooked Pete even if the war had been lost. But when Pete got out of his pen, he was especially mean to black people and she thought this was why her mother hadn't kept after Mr. Remmler about his poultry.

"Oh, merciful God," said Lena, looking toward the car coming down the street. "Now just look what you see." She straightened the hat on her head, and smoothing her dress, she walked across the yard and through the back gate, mumbling about black clouds settling on the day. "Some people's the same as bad weather. You just hope it don't stay long." Her voice trailed behind her like the thread of her unraveling hem.

Before Molly could focus both eyes on the car, Alfred shed some light. "Here come your grandparents," he said, surprised, since they rarely came to visit.

"My piano's coming," she explained, the excitement quivering in her throat like a bird tune. She looked over at Alfred to see if he'd noticed, but he was watching them through his hands, which he held like binoculars.

"Mmn." He pretended to see something that wasn't there just to annoy her she guessed, and went on adjusting his make-believe lenses. "They're old as Methuselah," he said.

So he did know something about the Bible. Knowing what he knew at the age of five was plain irritating. She remembered the very day he was born, but sometimes he seemed older than she was.

"I already knew you were getting a piano," he said. "Every-body does." He was also an eavesdropper.

Overhead, rafts of clouds collided and hung together. Just then she wasn't at all sure she really wanted the piano. "Grand-mother Willie wants to see it," she said, mostly to herself. Folding her fingers into the "here's-the-church" position, she wished to the Holy Ghost that Willie hadn't come.

Chapter THREE

Her grandparents' dusty black Ford rattled up the driveway, the bobbing of their old wrinkled faces a testimony to the ruts in the gravel that Nat was supposed to have raked smooth. Willie got out of the car and came round. Her shoulder dipped in sharp angles each time her cane poked the ground. The only time she seemed to need the cane was at the Flanagans' house. Molly's father said the cane was Willie's protection against the unholy ground of Nate Flanagan. As she stood under the elm holding the cane by the throat like a staff, Willie looked like Bo Peep gone gray. Each time she tamped one of the big roots that ran above ground a loud booming sound filled Molly's head, but Alfred was unaffected and didn't seem to hear it at all. He was busily digging his way to China, as he said, and Molly hoped he wouldn't find Hell instead.

Not wanting to confirm her suspicion of evil, Molly had never told her grandmother about the snakes. She also didn't want Willie to know that her father had not been able to get rid of them. Before her prayers had been answered by the Holy Ghost, she had wondered, time and again, if this ground *was* cursed with wickedness.

Molly waved just as she was supposed to do, but felt no love or kindness in her fingertips, only the fluttering awareness that

Willie was in the yard and black rain clouds were gathering over the Mississippi River to the west.

"Storm's brewing," said Willie, looking at Grandaddy Bob for assurance. He was as bald as President Eisenhower and pink as a pig. He got out of the car and looked toward the sky. Willie bragged on the accuracy of his forecasts, though no one had ever heard him utter a word about weather or much of anything else. Possibly the prognostications were registered in the depth of his blue eyes, measured by the width of his smile or monitored by the occasional twitch of an ear. Willie would stare into his face, read the signs and plan accordingly.

"I hope your grandfather hasn't brought you any more of that cow stuff," Alfred said. But Alfred's curiosity was replaced by irresponsible digging. He was flipping dirt all over himself and Molly. His lake was deep as a grave.

He'd been exposed to cow manure for the first time when he helped her plant the iris last spring. He was still upset that manure came from an orifice so close to the ones that gave milk. He no longer drank milk at all.

"C'mon," she said. Molly walked toward her grandparents, brushing the dirt from her green jeans. Alfred trailed behind.

Grandaddy Bob opened the trunk of the car and hoisted a bushel of peanuts and set it on the ground. Her grandparents had lived in Memphis for a long time now, but Grandaddy Bob drove down to their place on Bullfrog Corner in Horn Lake, Mississippi, almost every day to be with his cows. He never came over to the Flanagans' without an offering—turnip greens, rutabagas, okra, or some other vegetable with a strong taste.

Except for the small peanut patch, he didn't grow things himself, being solely involved with animal husbandry. But people down in Horn Lake generously shared their produce, so he ended up with more food than he and Willie could eat. Molly guessed her mother hadn't lived down there long enough to pick up the trait of sharing. She resented people borrowing ingredients, even though the sugar and flour that Charlotte's mother or Mrs. Flynn or Miss Doyle or Frances Mahon returned always had a pinch more than they'd gotten and, added together, they made up for what Ludie Finch never gave back.

"Is it here yet?" called Grandmother Willie.

"No, ma'am," she said, feeling sort of white and woolly under Willie's tense black eyes. "In a few minutes, I think." Molly's progress in music had not been as great as the other granddaughters' and Willie had grown impatient with the Flanagans about getting the piano. She was so sure they'd not buy it and that Molly would not be ready for the recital in December, that she hadn't bothered to assign her piece. But sooner or later she'd get around to it. Suddenly Molly realized that along with the piano would come hours of practice. Her performance at the recital would now be judged the same as the other granddaughters' who already owned pianos—her mistakes as black as mortal sin and less forgivable. On recital day, Willie's hair would be combed back of her ears so as not to miss a single note.

Nat swung open the screen door at the side of the house, and looked at the peanuts, enough for a herd of elephants. "Goobers. Good Gooooodness. Wait 'til Dad sees this," he said.

He had almost slipped and said "God" in a way that would have undermined Willie's good opinion of him. Molly felt herself wishing he'd done it. She pictured him disguised as Planters Mr. Peanut.

"For the whole family," snapped Grandmother Willie, her voice suggesting that her father, with his fondness for nuts, might selfishly eat the whole bushel himself.

Grandaddy Bob gently cuffed Nat on the shoulder without a word. Two or three times a year—amazing when it happened— he'd fool you and speak. Molly would hear his soft voice and jump with surprise, the same as when Nat came up behind her and screamed.

Her father opened the louvered door and stepped outside. "Mother Willie," he said as though her name were the title of a poem he planned to recite. Molly was certain that Edgar Allan Poe or Henry Wadsworth Longfellow never wrote about Baptists, although Walt Whitman might have stuck one in somewhere. Giving Willie a half-bow, her father shook hands with Grandaddy Bob, then picked a handful of peanuts from the basket, putting them in his pocket.

"The pecans are already sacked up, Mr. Bob." The pecan trees in the backyard were laden with nuts. They traded pecans and peanuts every year. Grandaddy Bob smiled widely. Molly was just as sure he liked her father as she was that Grandmother Willie didn't.

Her mother came on out wearing a dress way bigger than needed. Grandaddy Bob hugged her, almost a nuzzle really, which slightly embarrassed Molly. This greeting seemed private.

Then Willie nodded to her daughter. "Elizabeth," she said. Not "Hello, Elizabeth" or "Howdy, Elizabeth" or "How are you, Elizabeth." Just plain "Elizabeth." Elizabeth Flanagan greeted her mother with a slight touch on the shoulder, then coughed to the side.

All of them started talking. They went on and on about Nat's straight As in school, his talent for football and acting, and how ambitious he was with his paper route. When they took up with Molly's wandering eye, she felt it going off on its own. They discussed how the optic exercises were taking a long time for results. They talked about the possibility of an operation.

"No need for it," said Willie. "The Lord sends signs to remind us all of our imperfections. She'll learn to tolerate adversity same as the rest of us." She looked at Jim Flanagan.

"No need for a handicap when there's a way to fix it," he said. "We're made in the image and likeness of God. I doubt His eyes are going off in two different directions. The operation's a simple adjustment."

No one seemed to notice her standing right there. She felt a slow burn behind her eyes. What they failed to realize was seeing two things at the same time was a gift, a talent none of them owned or even imagined, not even Nat. Right now Willie was on the periphery of her left eye, looking haggard from reading the small print of her Bible, while her father, in full view of the right eye, was handsome though dirty from trying to mend the fence that persisted in leaning in spite of his efforts.

"How will you pay? Doctors don't come cheap."

"Not to worry yourself, Mother Willie," he said. "Business isn't great, but there's the rental property."

"From one of *those* places. Evil *begets* evil. 'Vengeance is mine'—that's what the Lord said and that's what He'll take."

Heat lightning flashed inside Molly's head. So that was it. Her father would pay the doctor with rent money from the old building he'd inherited, and she'd have to take the rap for the sins of the Flanagans. She closed her eyes and imagined herself blind.

Grandaddy Bob's head nodded toward Willie chin first, as if to nudge her over the stile and onto another subject. Molly wanted to call him Pinky.

Willie hooked the cane over her wrist. The vein that ran down her hand was a blue River Niger. "Who's toting the piano? Nigras?" Neither Willie Hardy nor her daughter Elizabeth Flanagan could pronounce "Negro." Lena didn't like the way they said it; Molly could tell by the look on her face. Willie said, "City Nigras every bit as lazy as ones from Mississippi. Lazier'n Bob's cows." Grandaddy Bob blew his nose to protest the insult to his livestock. "Just hope you got steady ones," she said, doubting anyone here was, least of all Negroes.

"It's coming by way of a couple of big palooka friends of mine," said her father. "They're a little on the slow side, but we tied a string onto the van so they could find the way back." He explained this with only the slightest smile on his face. The palookas were Tim and Tom Flynn, a fireman and a policeman ordinarily, who moved things on their days off. They were the sons of Mrs. Flynn next door. "If they refrain from making too many stops along the way, we'll have ourselves a musicale." He sounded uncertain about the stops. Tim and Tom had a penchant for bourbon.

"Ready, Molly?" She could tell that her father wanted to make a celebration of the new used piano. Impossible, Molly thought, now that Willie was here.

Getting her own piano was too much to think of and she tried hard not to think of it. She'd always hated unwrapping presents in front of people and would find ways to save them for later when she could be alone. In her own room with a gift, anticipating its unveiling, she was King Midas clutching gold. Any minute now the moving van would pull up in front of the house and she would have to share the first sight of her piano, a rare golden moment, with her family as well as the whole neighborhood.

"When they get round to bringing it," said Willie with characteristic impatience, "we might all be dressed in our funereal clothes." She was looking toward Alfred's big hole. Her glasses slipped down on her nose and stayed there like two headlights aimed at the ground. Her stance in that black dress prompted Molly to wonder two things: if the dead kept their glasses; if she would cry at Willie's funeral.

The FLYNNS HAUL ALL turned the corner three blocks away. The old white van sputtered and backfired as it started slowly up the street.

"Here it comes," said Alfred.

"Maybe," said Nat.

The van bucked, then stalled at the next intersection.

Through the windshield the Flynns' red hair caught Molly's eye like cardinals in snow.

Screen doors hawed as the neighbors assembled to watch. The van stopped in front of the house, then backed up to the curb with a screech, the piano jangling as it bumped against the rear doors that flew open with the impact. The piano was held in by a rope that stretched across the opening. Tim and Tom were in no hurry. They sat inside the cab eating sandwiches from a brown sack and drinking milkshakes from paper cups, stoking themselves for the work of hauling the piano inside.

Willie looked disgusted. "Those two are sorry sights. They could at least wait supper 'til after the work's done."

"Mother Willie, Tim and Tom are the sons of our neighbor," said Molly's father as though Tim and Tom were celebrities. "Strapping lads. Once they start they'll get the job done posthaste. With the Flynns it's all a matter of careful planning," he said, knowing full well that the Flynns never planned anything. The movement of their lives was directed by food, talk, bourbon, and happenstance. Molly thought that their red hair might be achievement enough, like the end of a fall day when the sun is truly beautiful and wild. But she did wish they'd hurry it up.

Stretching and yawning, Tim and Tom finally got out of the van. Squat and burly, they both looked poured into navy blue pants that strained hope. They reminded Molly of Snoop Wiggly and Wiggly Snoop in a book she'd read a long time ago. After a long discussion, they rolled the piano down a board ramp that threatened to buckle under the weight. Molly held her arms tightly as if she might keep the balance and prevent the piano from smashing to smithereens.

Molly wished she had the chance to see her own piano without the whole world watching. But there it was—an upright made of mahogany, the front burled, the grain like a swirling melody. With Tim at the bow, Tom at the stern, the piano teetered and rocked as they plowed through the yard and up the steps. Hammers fell on the wires, volunteering a haphazard melody. Lena held the door for them and hummed "Bye and Bye."

"Up she goes," said Tim. The men grunted as they carried the piano over the threshold, both of them puffing mightily. Everyone followed them inside. Alfred laughed discreetly when Tim farted. In the living room, they bumped the piano into the Victorian settee that no one but ghosts ever sat on. Instantly Molly heard the frank clearing of a throat, most likely a protest from Grandfather Nate over Willie's presence. Willie glanced up at St. Cuthbert and shook her head. Just then Molly thought the otters seemed particularly vicious.

"So that's where," said Nat as they angled the piano through the narrow hall bloomed out in pink cabbage roses. They set the piano down hard on top of the floor furnace and rested a minute, rubbing their hands. Together they took in deep breaths, yelled "heave ho!" then picked it up and stumbled through the doorway. When they dropped the piano in Molly's bedroom, the whole house vibrated.

"You've notified the piano tuner, haven't you now, Elizabeth?" Willie's voice was streaked with doubt. Several keys on her own piano were silent, but she claimed she was waiting until just before the recital to have them fixed. When it came time to pay, her mother and Willie were both Scotch as all get out. Neither of them favored the eye operation, but for all that was said about God's will, money—whether ill gotten or hard earned—was most likely the real reason.

Ordinarily Tim and Tom would stay and swap stories with her father, but after meeting Willie, they opted instead to go on next door. "Aunt Doyle's waiting with the rice pudding," said Tim, apologizing for leaving so soon. Molly wondered if he would have his bourbon along with the pudding.

Everyone gathered in her bedroom to inspect the piano. Her father asked, "Might we have the pleasure of a tune, Mother Willie?"

Molly struggled inside of herself, but after a moment forgave him. There really wasn't any other choice but to invite Willie to play the piano first.

Quickly Willie got down to business. "'What a Friend We Have in Jesus,'" she announced. Molly wondered why she chose that one, since her favorites were "The Old Rugged Cross" and "Amazing Grace." After playing only a few bars of the hymn, she turned and looked at Molly's mother. "Why Elizabeth," she said, her mouth full of awe, maybe even a little forgiveness, "the tone's as good as any."

Elizabeth Flanagan's eyes widened with wonder. The apprehension fell from her face. Willie kept on playing, really enjoying herself on Molly's new used piano. She ended the hymn with a flamboyant trill, surprising even herself, the expression of delight that swept across her face as welcome to everyone as rain in a desert. When she got well into "A Closer Walk with Thee," Lena started humming along and soon Nat and her father were swaying in time. Grandaddy Bob's Adam's apple pulsed a little. Elizabeth Flanagan had withdrawn to stand in the no-man's-land of the doorway, neutral in her silence.

Satisfied with the piano, Willie stopped playing and settled herself. "Molly, you've got the means to the end now. No excuses."

Molly didn't recall ever giving any. It wasn't her way. But she said nothing.

"Wash the ivories with Ivory soap," Willie commanded. "Tepid water's best." She pointed her forefinger down as if testing the temperature of the water.

"Yes, ma'am." Molly was thinking how Willie herself never washed anything. Even now her ears could stand a good cleaning.

Nat said, "What about the mandolin attachment?"

"Not now," said Elizabeth Flanagan, staring him down. She looked as if she would surely strangle him if he were one step closer. She was twisting the red dishtowel.

Her father didn't get it. "Oh, by all means. Let's have a mandolin tune."

"Later," said her mother, stalling. Her voice went higher the way it always did when the one word stood for a whole sentence. "It's Wing and Son. Did I tell you what a good buy it was?"

"What about this attachment?" Willie refused to advance

toward brand name or price. Leading with her nose, she stood up to prevent the shuttling aside of her question. Her eyes, fixed on her daughter's, were wily and true like a hawk's.

Elizabeth Flanagan's eyes narrowed in a brood. She was trapped. "I don't remember exactly how it's done," she hedged.

Nat pulled up the heavy front lid, exposing the hammers and wires. "What now?" He was Sherlock Holmes, investigating.

"Oh, turn one of the handles," she admitted with a deep sigh. "I don't remember which one." She was pointing a finger, but with a slack hand.

As Nat sat on the bench and began fumbling with the metal bars underneath the keyboard, her father was talking to Grandaddy Bob about football, a subject Grandaddy Bob probably knew little about, so absorbed was he with heifers, calves and bulls, and the price of feed. But always they were anxious to please one another and Grandaddy Bob listened intently. Their friendship lifted—if only for a few moments—the heavy hand of religion.

Her father paused and looked at her. "Go ahead, Molly," he said, motioning her to sit down. He seemed the only one to remember that the piano was hers. "Give way to Molly, Nat," he said in his ship captain's voice.

Before he scooted over, Nat found the handle and turned it. Inside the piano two horizontal bars shifted the felts in front of the wires, constricting the hammers. He lowered the lid. Molly sat down and played a few bars of "Minuet in G," easily ignoring her own mistakes because of the wonderful and unique tinkling sound of the mandolin.

"It sounds like a harpsichord, doesn't it, Elizabeth? Mozart's instrument!" Willie approved of Mozart and clapped her hands hard together one time, an enthusiasm that was startling. Her face cracked a smile. That she liked the piano felt good.

"Why, yes. Yes, it does sound that way." Elizabeth Flanagan's answer was slow in coming, but she, too, was smiling. The burden had lifted and she tossed her head back and seemed to relax.

Molly felt safe in her mother's calm, the relief like after a tornado has passed over. And maybe Willie really had forgiven her mother. Maybe she'd forgiven them all.

Fascinated by the sound of the piano, Nat was still sitting beside Molly. He never had to practice. He could play by ear. "Listen to this," he said. He elbowed her aside and got going. Grinning his head off, he played a rumbling boogie-woogie, his fingers walking wickedly on the lower keys the way Benny Frenchie had done in the old days down at the Nonpareil. (Molly knew that as a boy her father had stood outside the saloon, listening. His father had forbidden him to go inside.) The music was jumping and Alfred couldn't keep still. He humped his shoulders—grooving, jiving, and snapping his fingers.

Like a railroad man signaling a train with a bright flag, Molly's mother waved her red dishtowel at Nat, hoping to avoid the disaster that was rolling in with rhythmical momentum.

"Devil's music," said Willie straight out. She held her hands knotted out in front of her, like she was carrying a sign. "Out of a saloon and where'd you learn such a thing, Nat?" But before he could answer, she said, "Jim Flanagan, you're the one waging for sin. From one of those places."

Her father was amused, but tried to look serious for her mother's sake. "Well, it does have a bit of a flair, now doesn't it?"

"For their vine is of the vine of Sodom, and of the fields of Gomorrah, their grapes are grapes of gall, their clusters bitter." Willie was a black bird now, a crow. She'd flown straight out of Deuteronomy.

"Ain't that the truth," said Lena. "And more so they wine is the poison of dragons, they sho is, and the cruel venom of the asps. That there piano's witnessed the Playin' of the Dozens. Sure to have seen sinful comings and goings, I'm here to tell you." Once she got to talking, she just couldn't seem to shut up. Her voice sounded joyful. Any minute now she might sing. "Those places of Mr. Flanagan's done seen some kind of times. Rolling barrel-houses. That's what."

Molly could see that her mother wanted to fire Lena on the spot, but it would serve no purpose. The damage had been done.

She was wondering if Lena had ever been in one of those places when Willie looked her in the eye and said, "Molly girl, wash the whole piano with the Ivory. Inside and out. After that, see it's altogether dry." Almost to herself she said, "Warped already's my guess." She was talking to Molly, but at the same time looking at Jim Flanagan and puffing. "And don't you be practicing with that attachment, hear me?"

"Yes, ma'am," she said, knowing full well that as soon as

Willie left she would play everything she'd ever learned with the bar turned for the mandolin sound. Would Grandmother Willie ever leave?

An explosion of loud voices from across the street quickly led all of them to the window. Mr. Finch stood in their yard yelling at Mrs. Finch, who was swinging a black iron pot back and forth like a pendulum.

"She's a lefty, Dad," said Nat.

Mrs. Finch spit on the ground. "You little bastard!" she yelled.

"She calls him 'little' when she wants him mad," said Alfred, happily. "She's going to kill him with that pot."

With a broad smile on his face, her father said, "Alfred, if Mrs. Finch hits target, it wouldn't kill Harry Finch anyhow—the spirits he consumed will save him."

Molly wasn't sure about the spirits, but thought Mr. Harry Finch plain lucky to be a foot shorter than his wife, which meant he didn't have to duck if she heaved the pot. Molly's mother started coughing, her face burning red. Molly's own face felt warm. "I hope she misses him," she blurted, wanting to apologize to Willie for the neighbors' behavior.

Mr. Finch shifted side to side, flailing his arms, bobbing and weaving. "Good footwork," said Nat. "The Artful Dodger. He should rush her."

Molly thought the slightly built Mr. Finch was too afraid to do any such thing, but suddenly he seemed to grow larger as the timbre of his own voice swelled loud as a trumpet. He stood still and, like a little red-nosed clown, pointed his fingers at his head, offering himself as a fixed target. "Ludie, damn you

woman—for once in your life do something half-assed right!"
he yelled. He begged her to hit him. Her arm, arcing wide with
the momentum, let go of the pot, which spun round and round,
sailing over his head before hitting the ground like a meteor.
"Stupid bitch!" he hollered.

"Missed by a mile," said Nat, sounding his disappointment,
but his voice sounded uneven as he said it. Molly looked to see
if he would say more. She knew he was worried for Jane.

"Witnessing such carrying on bodes ill for these children,"
said Willie. "And for you, too, Elizabeth." She didn't mention any
possible bad effects on Molly's father. Her sensibilities seemed
frazzled, her face full of grief. "How long do these rows go on?
The police should stop them."

"When you get divorced," said Alfred with the confidence of a
teacher, "you go to church and wear black and the priest says
you aren't married anymore."

"Where'd you get such a notion?" asked Willie, seriously
wanting to know.

"Jane said."

"Jane?" Grandmother Willie questioned everything but the
Bible and the Reverend Billy Graham.

"Jane's a dancer," confessed Nat with a knowing look.

"A neighbor." Molly didn't want Willie to start up about the
evils of dancing. She herself dreamed of dancing and did not
want Willie to influence her mother against it. Standing there in
her room, crowded and barely able to breathe, Molly wished her
grandparents hadn't migrated from Mississippi.

Finally the rain began its patter and put out the Finch family fire. Mr. Finch slogged toward his car. After shaking his finger at Mrs. Finch, he got in and drove away.

The Finches were Catholics. As far as Molly knew, Catholics never divorced, but divorce couldn't be as bad as murder. She was glad Willie didn't know to what religion the Finches belonged.

Mrs. Finch picked up the iron pot and went inside. It seemed unlikely that she'd cook in it now. Ray Finch followed her, cracking his knuckles. Jane looked jittery sitting there on the steps in the rain, jingle-jangling her tap shoes, and staring after her father as if he'd suddenly erased a blackboard full of instructions. Nat watched her intently.

Molly guessed feelings could be as big as a person. And seeing Sue and Jimmy crouched behind the porch rails, growling and pretending they were tigers in a circus wagon, she thought that being small was probably best.

The rain gave her grandparents an excuse to leave. She watched them hobble across the wet ground toward the car, Willie poling herself forward with her cane that sank into the evil mud. Molly was quite glad to see them go, though in the commotion, Willie had forgotten to assign her recital piece. She was hoping for "Minuet in G" or "Londonderry Air" or perhaps even the "Tarantella."

Alfred sat down on the piano bench. With his hands arched like a concert artist's, he played "Chopsticks" without the mandolin attachment and kept perfect time. The tune needled her ears. At the recital, maybe she'd just play that.

Chapter FOUR

"Just don't you be making it too long a time, you hear?" Lena's voice squeezed through the louvers. Molly was taking a break from practice, sitting very still on the damp front steps and looking out from within herself.

Most likely Lena was wanting her to get on with it so they'd have time for art. Lena could draw anything that lived. She would sketch the neighborhood on butcher's paper, then the two of them would label everything. Lena depended on Molly for the correct spellings. The bayou was named the River Jordan; the Wolf River that it flowed into, the Dead Sea. Along the banks of the Jordan—really the Flanagans', Flynns', Mr. Remmler's, and the Colberts' backyards without any fences, clotheslines or doghouses—she would draw camels, donkeys, and birds indigenous to the Holy Land. The people in her sketches, both black and white, wore robes like Moses and Jeremiah.

Grandmother Willie was big on the Bible, too, and filled most of Molly's time with talk of it. At piano lessons when Molly paused between tunes or held a whole note, Willie would slip in a snippet about Absalom or Solomon. But it wasn't the same thing with Lena. Lena didn't talk Bible much. She grieved to be *in* it, so much so that she just drew herself there. And she would always take Molly along. There they'd be, feeding straw to the camels or leading a donkey to the well. Molly always stood beside Lena in the drawings, both looking as biblical as Ruth and Rebecca. The only things not biblical were Molly's blue glasses and Lena's umbrella, an arc of rainbow colors. Lena allowed Molly to paint the stripes of the umbrella in bright reds, greens, and blues, but made her leave their robes white.

Green leaves from the trees looming overhead dripped water as vapor rose hot and alive off the street, black as a forest stream. The piano had been hers for several hours. She knew she was different and now was waiting to feel it. If she didn't move at all—like Mr. Remmler's cat, Sid—the feeling would come. Sid was hunched near Mrs. Flynn's downspout by a burrow, pretending sleep and all the while waiting for a mole to pop up from the hole and into his mouth. A mockingbird screamed and spoiled things, right as the mole's nose peeked out then disappeared with the sound. Sid arched his back and quickly traversed the flower bed on tiptoes, picking his feet up high as if the ground were a bed of red hot coals. Chuck Berry hollered "Maybelline" from Nat's record player.

The small porch on the side of the house, battened down and boarded up as a room for Nat, was part of the shuffling of things done to make way for the baby, Molly guessed. Her mother had shrugged off the loss of the porch, saying that she knew more about what was going on in the neighborhood than she wanted and she had no desire to watch it. Elizabeth Flanagan never suspected the whole of it, nor would Molly ever tell her the secrets she'd come to know.

Across the street Mrs. Finch started for the Mahons'. Probably she knew better than to wear her flowered apron in public, but it offered the convenience of a big pocket where she kept her Lucky Strikes, matches, and her pink rosary.

Molly's mother smoked only one Camel per night. This was probably the reason she was never invited for coffee with Frances Mahon and Ludie Finch, who both smoked night and day like two smudgepots. If Willie found out about her mother's smoking, she would probably blame it on her father. If he got her to smoke more, Molly wondered would she have more friends?

Mrs. Finch was tall and lanky. She seemed in a trance as she flicked her cigarette and muttered the rosary. Mr. Finch had not yet returned and maybe that was the reason for the prayers. Molly wondered if she was praying for him to come back or stay gone. Either way, smoke from the bonfire of Hail Marys, burning down deep in her chest, billowed and streamed from Mrs. Finch's mouth.

Frances Mahon opened the door for Ludie Finch. Frances was short and sturdy, like a small overburdened donkey. The lump of baby under the blue smock arrived places seconds before she did. After a dozen or more childless years, the Mahons had received the gift of Alfred. Now they were hoping for a second miracle.

Nat was singing "That's All Right" along with Elvis. When he wanted, Nat could get his voice up high like that. In fact, there wasn't much Nat couldn't do. Always his talents cropped up as unexpectedly as dandelions. From behind his screen door, his black shadow darted and circled back on itself, like a panther in a cage.

Mrs. Flynn and Miss Anna Doyle, both of them plump, walked noiselessly along the edge of their porch, carrying cans with long spouts, watering what looked to be a hundred pots of African violets. The sisters waved at Molly, but ignored Mr. Remmler next door to them, though he bumped up and down on his yellow chair, tipping his cap like an organ-grinder's monkey. Molly's mother and the two old ladies kept their distance from Mr. Remmler, none of them wanting to associate with the poor. All three of the women, Miss Doyle, Mrs. Flynn, and Elizabeth Flanagan, suspected him of feeding pigeons—the full knowledge of which was a secret Molly shared with her father. Secrets were like old sets of china, they never wore out because they were never used. Molly had never told a secret.

"The pudding's made," called Miss Doyle, congratulating herself. "A big bowl just for you, Molly," chimed Mrs. Flynn. They celebrated good times with rice pudding. Miss Doyle played the air with her fingers. Both sisters seemed terribly happy about the piano.

Not much happened in the lives of the old people, and since they had no television sets, the three of them listened to or breathed in what spun off of the neighbors. Mr. Remmler was the more faithful observer, not bothered by rain, heat, or cold, and could have filled in the blanks of what the two women missed if they had asked him. Instead, they surmised, speculated, and imagined what had gone down.

A plumbing truck was parked in the Mahons' driveway.

Alfred came out of his house and stood there holding his nose. "The john's doing it again," he hollered, whether she wanted to know or not. She knew he was desperate for conversation, but she refused to encourage him. Still waiting to feel different, she was not moving a muscle. Only occasionally did she blink. Alfred gave up and started digging.

Like the Mississippi River, the john down in his basement flooded every so often. The Mahons referred to it as the "maid's toilet," but in truth Essie was afraid of the basement and wouldn't even open the door. "No time, no way, is Essie bumping into no snakes," she'd say.

The "maid's toilet" sat on a concrete platform a step up from the stone floor near the north wall, where the moss grew on the bricks, and just under the high window covered by an iron grating in a fleur-de-lis pattern. Before Molly had grown out of such things, she and Alfred had pretended that the commode was the throne of a great king. Wearing a sheet that his mother had obligingly dyed purple, Alfred had appeared regal sitting on the white porcelain pot holding his father's hammer painted gold like a scepter. Molly had wanted to call him "King Arthur." Alfred had accepted his crown of clover, but would tolerate no name other than his own.

Across the street Lonnie, the blind broom man, was tap-tap-ping his cane along the sidewalk, toting his bundle of brooms, selling house-to-house as he did every so often. Alfred stopped digging, waiting for Lonnie to come near, then went over and escorted him up the Mahons' steps. Like always, Frances came to the door and bought a broom to join the others piled in the basement. Lonnie held Alfred's arm as he walked back down the steps, then tapped his way to the next house. Molly closed her eyes, listening to his sound. Her own mother had one broom and "didn't need another." If Molly had the operation and ended up blind, she wondered if Alfred would guide her along the street as she sold her brooms, and if her own mother would buy one.

Alfred resumed his digging. "The Finches are getting divorced," he said, mud on his hands and knees.

She was glad when he spoke, glad not to have to think anymore about herself. "Where'd you hear such a thing?" She wasn't real sure about the particulars of divorce, but wasn't about to admit this to a five-year-old, even if he was a genius.

"Mrs. Finch said so. She's inside drinking coffee and smoking cigarettes with Mother," he said. She heard a tickling sound in his throat as if he'd inhaled their ashes. "She said she couldn't live with Mr. Finch anymore."

Molly guessed that he couldn't live with her either: Mrs. Finch's aim might improve; his leaving was no doubt a wise decision, even if it meant sin.

Shuffle hop step. On the porch of the airplane bungalow the other side of Mr. Remmler's, Charlotte Colbert tap danced behind the bamboo curtain. *Shuffle hop step step.* Charlotte had let her try on the tap shoes—way too small even though Charlotte was two years older. The August air hung heavy as dog breath. Patches of sky were the pale blue of summer's end. Molly shifted side-to-side, then rolled up the sleeves of her plaid shirt. Hot days were dancing by like girls on a stage. She felt the riddle of discontent, or maybe she was remembering the rest-lessness of fall when brown leaves spiraled from the trees, and soon it would be that way again.

At the Finches, Ray pushed Sue and Jimmy out the door and locked them out. They beat on the glass and yelled for Jane. Mrs. Finch leaned her neck out of the Mahons' door like a giraffe from a shelter and called to them in a voice that was raspy and short of breath. "Sue! Jimmy! What on earth?" But she quickly shut the door before they could answer. Molly watched the Mahons' house with her right eye, the Finches' with her left.

Suddenly Jane ran from around the side of the Finch house in a blur. Molly squinted and focused both eyes on her. Jane looked like a dancer even when she was running and dripping with sweat. She slowed in the front yard and walked lightly through the dust, her footprints like stepping stones behind her. Through the trees the golden light speckled her with what seemed a powerful promise. Sue and Jimmy ran toward her. She gathered them in her arms and the three of them sat on the steps. Jimmy wiped the dust from her tap shoes.

"Nat sings real good," hollered Alfred.

"Chuck Berry," said Molly, though she knew good and well that it was pure Nat. He was imitating Chuck Berry while he put on more records. If she listened long enough maybe she could learn to play "Maybelline." She might play it in the recital. She smiled at the thought.

Ray Finch stomped out on the porch, scowling. Sue and Jimmy ran into the yard. Jane quickly got up and began *shuffle hop step stepping* down her front walk. Ray seemed mad about the dancing. He slammed the door when he went back inside, so hard Molly was surprised the glass didn't shatter.

Nat stopped singing abruptly when he heard the Finches' door bang. Now the only sound was Jane's jingle taps. Nat let Elvis take over. "Blue Moon of Kentucky" echoed from his room. Jane might well have been on stage wearing a royal blue costume with red sparkles instead of her faded green shorts. Molly saw Nat's dark shadow fixed and unmovable on the screen door, like spatterwork. Jane's long legs were made for dancing. They were almost as long as the legs of the package of Old Gold cigarettes that danced on the Ted Mack Amateur Hour. *Shuffle hop step step, ball change.* Jane danced toward Charlotte's house, swinging her arms as she went. She was dancing slightly ahead of the fast music. Her thick dark hair swept side to side, brushing her shoulders. Then she reached out in front—one arm, then the other—up and up they went with each *shuffle hop step step*—her fingertips higher and higher, flickering as though touched with stardust. Mr. Remmler began to clap loudly, Mrs. Flynn and Miss Doyle more lightly, but both ladies were nodding with pleasure. Not one of them had ever shown such appreciation for Molly's piano playing. Suddenly she felt the difference; this was not the feeling she'd been waiting for.

Jane disappeared behind Charlotte's bamboo curtain and both sets of jingle taps shuffled almost in synch. Molly guessed it was Charlotte out of step. Elvis was singing "I'm Left, You're Right, She's Gone" when Nat turned down the record player.

Either Charlotte and Jane couldn't hear Elvis or they wanted to see Nat. They craned from behind the bamboo curtain like performers taking a head count of the audience. Again Nat watched from behind the screen door. His face looked as absent as a drifting cloud, but even from behind the screen, Molly could see his eyes burned with light.

Nat did not know that Jane was responsible for most of Molly's worldly knowledge, everything she hadn't learned from books. Jane had told her the thing she wasn't supposed to know a long time ago, so long ago that Molly couldn't remember a time when she hadn't known. It had seemed that Jane was trying to give away something that she didn't want, that if she told someone she could forget what she knew. Jane and Charlotte were almost the same age. If Charlotte knew what Jane did, she never said. When Jane would sing "Your Cheatin' Heart," Charlotte would huff and go home to her Nancy Drews. Charlotte said that only hicks like country music.

Molly was allowed to walk to the Rosemary Theater on Saturday with Charlotte, whereas going with Jane was "out." Elizabeth Flanagan would say "out" like an umpire in a ball game.

Watching Jane, Molly felt clumsy and now looked around the yard as if searching for grace. The rain came down, warm and stinging on her arms.

The door opened behind her. "You'll take sick sitting out in hot rain like that. Come on in here, Molly."

She glanced back at Lena, standing there holding the door. Her brown face was dewy with heat. "Was a time when I wanted a pair of gold tap-dancing shoes more than heaven itself. The Lord didn't see fit to make you no dancer nohow. Same as me." Lena always seemed to figure out what Molly was thinking, even from behind when their eyes hadn't touched. "Piano's in there. Nobody's playing it."

"Okay," Molly said. "I'm coming." Scales were running through her head, black and white, up and down. The piano had invaded her room and now sat in there solemn and solid as a squatter. Each day it would be there, unchanging, hammering her conscience. She moaned quietly as she trudged inside.

Chapter FIVE

In the living room her father was reading from *One Hundred and One Famous Poems*. He looked up and laid it aside as she came toward him. "Tell me, mon chérie, 'Is there—is there balm in Gilead?—tell me—tell me I implore!'"

"'Quoth the raven, "Nevermore,"'" said Molly, just as she had been taught.

"Most certainly they *is* balm in Gilead. Lots of it," said Lena. "Take it from me, Mr. Jim. Balm is *in* Gilead. Thank Jesus."

"Yes, yes, Lena," he said. "The gospel according to 'Hambone's Meditations,' I suppose."

"Not that old Hambone," she said. "Don't you be making fun of me, Mr. Jim."

"Lena, I never make fun of anyone I don't truly admire. The gospel according to Jim Flanagan."

The cartoon figure looked as friendly and wise as Uncle Remus, but it was clear to Molly that Lena was not fond of Hambone.

The living room was rosy brown and warm. Molly thought that the ghosts lolling about kept it so. Mama Jo was probably sitting beside Clare on the settee, with Nate Flanagan alone on the side chair, all of them keeping her father company. He sat in the green lounge chair with a bowl of pecans on his lap. "Poet and Peasant Overture" was playing on the phonograph.

Lena said, "No peanut shells in the house, Mr. Jim."

"Lord no, Lena, I'm not eating peanuts. Now stop your worrying. You hear?"

"Just seeing after you, Mr. Jim." According to Lena, something bad would happen if you left peanut shells around. The pecans had nothing ominous associated with them.

He was extending a pecan half to Molly. "Mon chérie."

"Mon capitan," she said as she curtsied, a ritual from as far back as she could remember. She took the nut from his hand.

"Lena worked herself to death polishing your piano," he said.

"I guess I should practice, then."

"Nevermore," said Nat. He was sitting on the floor studying his playbook. He'd won the part of a pioneer in a play that had to do with Memphis long before it was a city. The production was to be held in the outdoor theater called the Shell. Nat knew his lines flawlessly, but still he practiced all the time. She'd heard him recite so often she knew the lines, too—except for the last part, which he was keeping secret until the opening night of the play.

"Before the land was mapped and carved, the roving Chickasaws hunted the deer, possum, and raccoon here in the canebrakes. They quietly crossed creeks and swampland and forged through thick tangled undergrowth, their footsteps answered only by the hollers of the red-winged blackbirds."

Interrupting, her father said, "Nat, this isn't Shakespeare. Think in the vernacular. Daniel Boone or Davy Crockett. Or better still, Natty Bumppo."

"Tell that to the director, Dad." Then he started up again.

"They moved over the great fallen timbers that had been snapped by a hurricane and into the primacy of the shade belly of woods where the dewberry and swamp dogwood bore fat succulent berries that fed white-tailed deer and black bears and brown turkeys that in turn fed them and their women and their children."

Molly moved her lips as he spoke. "Cut it out," he said. "I only have another week."

Looking at her, he took a deep breath and pressed on. "From the forest floor poked may apple, trillium with white spring flowers that shone at dusk, the nettle, pawpaw with fleshy fruit, blood of the bloodroot, squirrel corn."

"You might as well speak the Algonquian language of the Penobscots," sighed her father. "At least lengthen the vowel sounds in 'blood' and 'bloodroot.'"

Nat's lips seemed more red when he said "blood." When he said "pawpaw" Molly thought he sounded about right, like a Natty Bumppo, but for the most part he was as high-toned as Hamlet.

"The center of the spirit world, deep in the green luminescence of the browse, bore hackberries, sycamores, and black gums and oaks, the thick foliage hiding secret hollows and holes."

When he got to the secret hollows part, she was listening completely.

"Lick Creek wandered deep into the woods, reaching cool fingers around pebbles and over rocks, the rivulets a light rushing sound that soothed the silvery creature of legend sleeping hard on a bed of moss that covered the deepest of the hollows." He paused and looked at her.

She waited for the creature of legend to come on out. She wanted the full description, its width, breadth, and height. And the color of its eyes. Instead Nat got up and took the script to his room. He came back immediately with the collection book for his paper route. "Natty Bumppo's off for bear," he said, stuffing the book in his back pocket. He picked up three pecans and juggled them.

Her father said, "You'll have to think up your own ending, Molly. Bumppo's left us hanging in suspense again." He gave her another pecan half. Nat seemed to be waiting for the gift of a whole one himself, but it wasn't offered. Molly ate the nut slowly, crunching loud, but Nat pretended not to notice. He walked back through his room and out the side door.

He delivered papers every day of the week and sometimes even threw Ray Finch's route when Ray went off with his father. Often Molly was awake in the dark early morning when Nat left. He went barefoot, even in the bitter cold, and she'd hear the slap of the screen door and then nothing. She would imagine the toughened soles of his feet stepping along the pavement into the long black silence, a thin stream of time that led away from home and back again. From behind trees and fences the lurking night prowlers watched. But nothing touched him as he folded the papers, packed them in his canvas bag and sailed them to each porch and stoop. Someday, at dawn and wearing shoes, he'd leave home once again; that would be for all time's sake. Even so, Molly was glad her father cracked nuts only for her.

" 'Keeping time, time, time, in a sort of Runic rhyme . . .' " Her father was reading "The Bells." He adjusted his voice so that each stanza had its own tone: low-down and mellow; rising to a menacing wrangle; rolling gloriously; moaning and groaning. A bell for every occasion and they all seemed to overlap so that in the end you couldn't tell if they rang out of happiness or sadness and maybe it was both.

The first strains of "Rosamunde" had sounded ominous; now the Allegro was leading to the bright ending. Her father played the records in a certain order; next, the "Ave Maria" would plop and spin. The record was warped, but he played it anyhow, listening until midway where the warp was most pronounced and the distortion of violins intolerable.

A knock on the door drew Lena to open it. "Last bell," said her father. He closed the book and stood to greet Godmother Byrd as she walked in. Her chauffeur, Charles, drove her all over Memphis most every Saturday and oftentimes she'd visit. Today she seemed nervous and fretful. There was a stirring of ghosts, though no one but Molly seemed to feel it. Clare Flanagan had been Byrd's best friend.

"Come in. Come in," her father was saying, looking behind her for Charles.

"I told Charles to keep the motor running. Something's happened, but I'll get to that in just a moment. I've brought your dear mother's recipe for Southern Comfort I promised you. Let me just read it now while I've still half a mind. Oh hello, Molly dear." She looked Molly directly in the eyes like a surveyor. She was in favor of the operation, but never talked of it. Molly looked at her nose and saw only one.

The phonograph needle had worked its way toward the warp and now the music was eerie, as though the musicians hadn't bothered to tune their instruments. Molly could tell the sound grated on Byrd.

"Jim, I really must replace that record for you. The 'Ave Maria' ought to be sung, anyhow. It's just not the same without lyrics."

He walked over and mercifully rejected the record.

Byrd sighed relief and fumbled in her handbag. Perfume in the air seemed to speak as she found the yellowed paper and unfolded it. He reached out for the recipe, but she refused to give it to him until she'd properly explained the procedure.

"You place one bushel of dead ripe peaches in a stone crock and mash them to a smooth pulp, then add two tablespoons of brown sugar, two combs of honey, and a bit of yeast. Stir it with vigor . . . ; then you pour in six quarts of bourbon whiskey."

"Lord God," he said. He bumped his forehead with the butt of his hand.

"Mr. Jim, I hope you not planning to drink none of that," said Lena from the dining room where she was running the dustmop under the table.

"Well, it does sound somewhat stout. Mightn't we just dilute it a bit?"

"Follow it *exactly*," Byrd warned. She was the master brewer of a potion that might lose its magic in the hands of an amateur. "Cover the crock with heavy muslin, then tie it down hard. Put on the lid and seal it. You must bury the crock three feet deep for at least three weeks or longer." She looked up. "I bury mine in a barrel of sand in the basement."

"We don't have a basement because of the bayou. No doubt George Mahon'll help us drink it, so I'll ask him to keep the concoction down in his basement. Now what's all this other?"

She carefully folded the recipe. "Where's Elizabeth? We mustn't alarm her."

"Not feeling well. She's resting." Molly thought he seemed somewhat glum, but Byrd didn't press him for details.

"Well, I must tell you. Unbelievable is the word for it." She waited until all eyes were on her. Lena pushed the dustmop into the doorway.

"They came to the house early this morning with the news . . . from the zoo. Two men. Knocking on the door like they'd break it down! Well, they woke me out of a perfectly good dream and I had to find my robe and slippers. My word, it does seem careless . . . they've misplaced a python! All twenty-five feet of it."

"Oh, is that all?" he said. "They forgot where they put a twenty-five foot python? My word," he said, mimicking her. "It's just typical of something they'd do, is it not? You can't count on people these days."

"Jim Flanagan, for heaven's sake," said Byrd. "This is a most serious affair. They paid a call on each house bordering the zoo to warn us. I'm not really supposed to be telling this," she said, looking at Molly as if she were a fellow conspirator. "They don't want to cause panic or anything. But I felt strongly that it was my duty as godmother to let you all know."

"Then you've told no one else?" he asked. He winked at Molly.

"Only a few friends," she admitted. "Very close friends."

"You're not going to tell more?"

"Well, maybe one or two."

"I wish you'd take it all back, Miz Maclaurin," said Lena. "Every last word."

"If only I could, Lena. I truly would."

"Let's not worry over the thing. They'll find it soon enough." Her father motioned Byrd toward the settee, unaware that it was occupied. "Sit and talk for a while. Molly's gotten the new piano. She'll play for you."

Byrd quickly tucked the recipe into his shirt pocket and moved toward the door. "That's very kind. But I really must go. They say there's no real danger, mind you. But I'd feel better settled in."

Listening to Molly play was undoubtedly a sacrifice that Byrd offered to God, thereby gaining an indulgence, but today Molly could see she just wasn't up to it. She smoothed the white hair beneath the brim of her black straw hat, pausing long enough to hear the first strains of the overture of "Romeo and Juliet." "Work hard on your music, dear, and someday you'll study at the Conservatory. You'll play the 'Ave Maria.'" She stepped outside where Charles was waiting.

Molly heard the grinding of rocks as the car backed down the driveway. She doubted she'd ever play the "Ave Maria." In the first place, Willie had already counseled her against worshiping the Blessed Virgin. Secondly, she'd never be accepted into the Conservatory.

"Mr. Jim, you don't think Miz Maclaurin's gone crazy, now do you? Seems so to me. All that foolishness about the snake."

"Byrd never was one to waste a dramatic opportunity, Lena. Go on and finish your work. And don't either of you worry over this. She's given to coloring things somewhat."

And then to himself, he said, "Nat's play might turn out to be more real than we'd have imagined."

As far as Molly was concerned, the play's ending could be no worse than her old nightmares. She wasn't the least bit afraid as she went to practice. Snakes never had been a problem in daylight.

LENA WELCOMED dust as a "fine gift from God," and let it build up for as long as she could get away with it. In Molly's room, she was drawing a map on the floor with the dust mop. "This here's Egypt," she said. And with a downward motion she split it with the Nile. Whenever time ran short for unrolling the butcher paper, she'd use whatever surface was available, often a mirror or a tabletop. Today it was the floor. As if to size up her own cartography, she stepped inside Egypt and turned round and round.

She drew the Sinai Peninsula and was finishing up the Red Sea when Elizabeth Flanagan came in and placed a stack of clean clothes on the bed. She left the room without a word, her chest full of turbulence. The suppressed coughs escaped in pairs, her way of issuing a complaint to Lena.

Lena erased the whole Middle East with wide sweeping strokes. She pushed the dustmop out into the hall and shut Molly's door. "Miz Flanagan, you supposed to stay off of your feet," Lena said. "That's what the doctor done said anyhow."

Outside, the rain pelted the ground, slowly filling Alfred's gravesite, washing away Molly's village. The muddy water trickled across the sidewalk and into the gutter. And Lena was right. Molly *was* too old for making miniature worlds out of dirt. Then again she saw little difference between her own muddy constructions and Lena's aspirations. Clearly Lena would never actually set foot in the Holy Land.

Alone with the piano, Molly fumbled through the scales with the enthusiasm of buttoning a row of buttonholes or counting telephone poles from a car window. "Scales the same as bones." Willie had said this over and over again. "If you don't commit to them, your music'll be spineless as a kitten." Though Molly tried to pretend otherwise, her music lacked bones. Now that she had the piano, the obligation to master the scales was hers.

To relieve the boredom, she pretended her fingers were mountain climbers in the Swiss Alps, carrying a pack, a pick, and a rope. Each scale was a new peak to conquer—stepwise upward and yodeling, then downward, listening for the echo. When she stumbled, the rocks slipped from under her feet, plummeting miles downward, pocking the earth below with moon-like craters that soon filled with melted snow. Moving in from the distance, the recital loomed as a black cloud full of lightning and thunder. Before she could scale the peak of Mt. E-flat, her mother again opened the door of her bedroom and in came Charlotte.

She wore loafers today, but that didn't lighten the fact that she had new tap shoes tied with white satin bows in her closet at home. The tapping sound always led Molly's mind toward the

hot green sin of envy. (If not talented, Charlotte was at least dili-
gent, Molly would tell herself, attempting to thin her own dark
green jealousy.) Molly's mother had refused to consider dancing
lessons. If Molly went over her head to bring it up with her
father, silence would fill the house, making everyone tense and
wrung out. Grandmother Willie gave her the piano lessons for
free.

"*Tarzan.*" Charlotte announced the weekly feature at the Rosemary. She was in a hurry to get there, but stared at the piano
anyhow.

Molly's mother counted out fifty cents worth of nickels, then
recounted to make sure she'd not "given extra." Molly saw she
was pale and not feeling well—the baby again, but her mother
kept her problems to herself. Molly's father had little tolerance
for illness. When any one of them was sick, he would call the
doctor, then leave the house. Still, he wanted Molly's eyes
"brought to rein" and was pushing for the operation.

"Charlotte, have a hand at Molly's piano." Her mother was
generous enough when it came to something that couldn't be
used up. As Charlotte plopped down on the bench, Molly got
up and went to her dresser.

She picked up the comb and looked hard at herself in the
mirror. Her dark hair flipped up on one side, hung straight on
the other. She wished that it was the same on both sides. For a
moment the mirror held a distortion of images like a window in
heavy rain, the Baptist eye and the Catholic eye again going separate ways. She blinked and pulled them together.

The small scar on her forehead was a train track that shrank each year and would soon be gone. She remembered slipping in the puddle of water, splitting her head on the porcelain tub—her father driving the car like a madman, her mother pressing a rag to her bloody head in the back seat, while Nat, reaching over from the front seat, held her hand. Her father had been wild-eyed, unable to hear or speak, until after the cut was sewn and bandaged. She wondered, as she touched the scar, if those times held in memory would disappear along with it? This morning her mother and father had again argued over whether or not Molly should have the eye operation and again Elizabeth Flanagan had won, insisting that training the eye with exercises was the best treatment. Molly knew that money was the real reason, but she was glad not to have the operation because she knew her father would not stay in the hospital with her. She put down the comb and wondered who would fix her hair if she was blind.

Charlotte played "Chopsticks" with the rhythm of a tom tom. When she finished, Molly's mother clapped. Elizabeth Flanagan had a liking for Charlotte that sidestepped her normal mistrust of Italians. She refused to buy any more bread from the Tarantinos, Charlotte's grandparents, declaring that the last loaf she bought came over with Columbus. Molly had an idea her mother didn't approve of the Pope, either. Then again, Charlotte Colbert was only half-Italian.

"Come on," Charlotte said. "Now." Her voice was as harsh as a blue jay's, but not offensive enough to keep Molly from going with her to the movie.

Aside from dancing, Charlotte preferred lounging with her

Nancy Drews. Molly herself enjoyed reading—the one thing that could take you away from religion and everything else—but thought Nancy Drew and her predicaments were boring. The Flanagans owned the Edgar Rice Burroughs Tarzan books and she had read every one. Charlotte wouldn't touch a Burroughs, but she never missed a Tarzan movie. For a split second Molly wondered if the Tarzan books were available in braille.

As they left the house, Dr. Blasingame's car pulled into the driveway. She waved to him as they walked across the yard, suddenly knowing that this house call on a Saturday meant that her mother was worse off than she'd suspected. Maybe the responsibility for the baby growing inside of her had led her mother to take extra precautions, or maybe the baby itself was making her sick. A puzzle. As always, Molly easily assembled the border in her mind while the center pieces remained either scrambled or missing altogether.

To avoid Alfred—he would pester her to let him tag along—she urged Charlotte to walk faster, but just as they sped up, he hopped out in front of them from behind a hedge. "I lied," he said. "I told Mother you invited me to the show."

His honesty was hard to resist. She hitched her shoulders and looked at Charlotte.

"So long as he doesn't talk," she said.

Alfred got his money out of his pocket and handed it to Molly for safe keeping. "I shouldn't have done it," he admitted. She was thinking herself far too generous with Alfred, but took the money and motioned for him to follow. As they started walking, she glanced over at the Finches'. The house looked as empty and fragile as wet cardboard.

Down the street, they scooted by the bulldogs which snarled from behind Mr. Holcomb's chainlink fence—her father had said Mr. Holcomb behaved like a Nazi—and turned the corner where old Mrs. Morrow threw rocks and sticks at passers-by, all of whom she suspected of picking the round white blossoms from her snowball bushes. In truth, the evidence of flower petals dotted Alfred's shirt, which did not escape Mrs. Morrow's eye. She started hollering and throwing sticks from her porch, and one glanced off Alfred's shoulder. "I shouldn't have done that either," he said. The three of them quickly ran out of Mrs. Morrow's pitching range.

The street arched into a bridge over the bayou swollen with rainwater. A crow flew from the patch of Johnson grass growing as thick as bulrushes along the concrete wall above the water's edge. Molly stopped for a moment and watched the brown stream coursing toward the Mississippi River. Her father had said that Hernando De Soto first called the Mississippi the "River of the Holy Ghost." She imagined herself in a boat steered by the Holy Ghost surging southward to meet the oceans, a fearful reckoning with time, forever pulled by the mystery of the moon, but pushed, too, by powerful waves of hope.

Alfred pulled at her sleeve. Waiting at the other end of the bridge, Charlotte hitched her thumbs around her arms, drumming her fingers on her elbows. Across Jackson Avenue Charlotte's grandparents' store stood like a big drab box. Mr. Tarantino was holding the door open for Mr. Lonnie who was tapping up the steps. By the looks of his bundle, he hadn't sold but one or two more brooms since she'd seen him earlier.

Alfred forgot and waved to him. "If you tell Mr. Lonnie your birthday he'll tell you what day of the week you were born on. He doesn't have to think or anything. He just comes right out with it."

"You were born on a Friday," she said.

"That's what Mr. Lonnie said, too. What day for you?"

"Sunday," she said, wondering if that was why religion dogged after her every other day of the week as well.

Charlotte was waiting, patting her foot in waltz time.

"She's Monday, I bet," said Alfred out of the side of his mouth. "My father says that's just about the worst day there is."

Molly wondered what day her mother's baby would be born on. She hoped it wouldn't be on a Saturday when she was away at Willie's or the movies. In truth, she probably wouldn't know about it anyhow, not until they brought it home screaming. They'd hardly be able to keep a screaming baby a secret. She wondered, too, was the baby making her mother ill, or was the baby the one who was sick?

"This year." Charlotte was crinkling her forehead.

"Coming, hon," said Alfred.

"You know she hates that," said Molly. Charlotte had said waitresses and Mrs. Finch were the only ones to use such expressions—"lover" and "sweetheart" and "hon." Catching up with her, they crossed the street and headed toward the Rosemary Theater a few blocks away.

Chapter SIX

After squandering every penny on popcorn and Milk Duds, they found seats close to the movie screen. Alfred sat between Molly and Charlotte and ate popcorn from both their boxes.

The heavy red velvet curtain hanging in soft folds across the stage started things kicking around in Molly's head even before the movie began. She ignored Alfred's hand dipping in and out of her popcorn and imagined a recital—she stood up there on stage behind the curtain, wearing green and brown velvet leder-hosen, a hat stuck with an orange feather, and tap shoes tied with green satin bows, waiting for "The Happy Wanderer" to begin. Willie sat at the keyboard wearing a dress in the style of a Swiss housewife with puffed sleeves and a black apron. She cued Molly with a stern nod just before the start of her number—the tap dance, the yodeling, and then her finale—singing the chorus that sounded like laughter—but instead of getting on with it, Willie was arguing that they should both sing and play a duet— "Amazing Grace." Before anything was settled, the curtain slowly opened and two lions roared majestically.

As in Burroughs's books, the story progressed quickly. Drums beat in thumping rhythm, birds called mysteriously, and Pyg-mies chanted and danced with spears the size of arrows. Molly was becoming quite absorbed in the plot about white men trying to steal elephant ivory, when the person sitting next to her grunted. She felt his bulky presence without actually looking at him, the way Sid the cat looked at a cardinal, keeping her neck and shoulders straight, but watching him in the corner of her left eye. He wore a child's red stocking cap with a ball on top and made guttural sounds like pigeons make. When the elephants trumpeted, his own grunts raised in pitch and frequency becoming as wild as the night sounds she heard from the zoo when she stayed with Byrd.

Then Tarzan and Jane stood close together, her thin blouse wet and clinging, his shredded loin cloth slit and held on by a thin strip of hide. The awareness of the grunting man next to her faded as Molly's fear that Tarzan and Jane would disgrace themselves in front of the whole audience intensified. The palms of her hands knotted together and clasped over the box of Duds; her face was hot, and something strange welled inside her. She had the feeling that Alfred was far too young to be watching.

Just as *it* would happen, Cheetah bounded into the love nest, flapping his woolly arms, ruining the moment. At once the hulk beside Molly was flailing his arms and whopping her face with his stocking cap. She might well have been in the jungle facing a wild animal—*he was braying, screeching, hooting, then he roared* as she sat paralyzed in a blur of red wool, unable to move a muscle. Alfred steadied the popcorn, which was spilling, but did not seem otherwise alarmed, that is until Charlotte cocked her head like Pete and started pecking Molly with the voice she hated. "Why don't you do something, stupid?"

"She is not!" said Alfred, taking charge of the popcorn.

"You ought to tell the manager." Charlotte was a born stool pigeon.

Molly knew tattling was as bad as sin. But it was unlike Charlotte to call her "stupid," and Molly felt very much that way as they moved to seats on the side aisle. Just then she saw Nat sitting beside Jane five or six rows behind. Molly raised her hand and almost waved, but neither of them seemed to recognize her. Their faces were lit with yellow light, an immanence so startling that Molly felt suddenly afraid. She'd rarely seen them even talk to each other and now, with their heads together, almost touching, they appeared as actors in a movie. For a moment Molly wondered if the scene were real. Sin was in the air here. If they breathed too deeply, they'd fill up on it. She was mightily afraid they'd do what Tarzan and Jane had almost done.

"My mother said Jane's fourteen going on twenty-one," said Charlotte. "I don't think she looks older than me."

Charlotte wanted to hear that she herself looked older than fourteen, but in truth she looked her age and nothing more. Molly didn't say anything, only nodded her head slightly, which wasn't the same thing as a spoken lie. Then Alfred spoke up and clarified the situation with his little sharp sword of a tongue. "A lot younger than Jane. That's what you look like, Charlotte. Even younger than Molly."

Charlotte silently fumed, then turned sullen.

Rebuked by Tarzan, Cheetah had calmed down, tucking his head shamefacedly. Molly's skin still felt red. She looked over at the wild man and saw only a face full of nothing. His cheeks were puffy, his eyes slit like an Eskimo's. He was holding his arms, rocking back and forth, winded after acting like an animal. His tired cap sat limply on top of his round head.

"Ronnie Rosemary," said Charlotte, answering before Molly could ask. "They let him in free. He's going to die when he's fifteen."

"How old *is* he?"

"He might be that *now*."

Alfred was looking over at Ronnie. "He looks like he's going to cry. But he doesn't look sad."

In truth, he looked freakish. The seed that the Flanagan and Mahon babies might not turn out just right was planted in Molly's head. Mrs. Flynn and Miss Doyle had been knitting prodigiously. Having finished booties for both babies, they were now engaged in larger projects. Mrs. Flynn was three feet into a six-foot pink-and-white afghan because one of the babies was bound to be a girl and Miss Doyle was soon to complete the trim on a blue sweater and cap. Skeins of yarn and yards of ribbon were heaped in their parlor. They had plans for buntings and blankets. Molly pictured the baskets filled with baby garments, waiting in the shadows, like sadness. Time hovered like a specter.

The *World News* was starting up for the second time. Charlotte wanted to stay and watch the movie all over again. But the scene of a python squeezing a native to death had been terrifying to Molly and facing tonight's darkness with a double feature of snakes—this added to a head already stuffed with memories of the same—was out of the question.

"A python escaped from the zoo," she said, hoping to enlighten Charlotte without frightening Alfred. She was ready to get moving.

"It'll be dark soon," said Alfred, standing up. "If we hurry up, we might see it."

Charlotte shuddered. "Let's go."

As they walked up the aisle, the world seemed sluggish like a film in slow motion. Molly looked for Nat and Jane, but they had left—or else they'd moved to the other side, where it was too dark to see. Molly felt strangely disconcerted and was wishing she hadn't come. She held her breath and thought it was for them.

"Nat and Jane are getting married, aren't they, Molly?" Alfred was looking around for them too. "They might elope."

"They're too young to get a license, nitwit." Charlotte was on top of things before Molly got a word out. Molly was slow to speak, wondering if Nat was the one who had taught Jane everything she knew about sex—wondering if they'd done *it*. Molly wasn't supposed to know anything *about* sex, not even about her own mother's baby, let alone have to worry about a bastard. Jane had told her about that, too.

Outside, groups of moviegoers scattered toward home in all directions. The sky was gray with gloom. The rain had turned to mist. "Get under," said Charlotte, opening her umbrella.

Molly refused, pushing Alfred under instead. It wasn't kindness that kept her out. Always the rain brought new words and thoughts and she worried that the rain would not last long enough to feel them. The spindrift dampened her arms, raising chill bumps. Ahead of them, almost over the rise of the bridge, she saw Nat and Jane, walking very fast. Molly thought they were anxious to be alone together in the Finch house. She rolled down her sleeves and buttoned the cuffs.

"So what are you thinking?"

"Oh, Tarzan," said Molly, almost telling the truth. Charlotte was demanding as all get out. But she didn't talk much, always wanting someone else to do it for her.

"I was thinking about Ronnie," said Alfred as if someone had asked. "He's big, but he's still a baby anyhow."

He was right. Molly was glad she hadn't taken Charlotte's advice and complained to the manager. All men were not created equal: a thing she'd suspected, but had never before looked at straight on. She guessed that her wandering eye was to blame, since it rarely focused on the same thing at the same time as the good one. It took both eyes to see that God sometimes got distracted and failed to finish what He'd started. Ronnie hadn't known what he was doing when he hit her in the face. Besides, Cheetah was his hero the same as Tarzan was Molly's. Who could blame him for acting like a chimp?

Soon darkness would fall, but snake or no snake, Charlotte insisted on stopping at her grandparents' grocery store. Mr. Tarantino gave her free candy; Molly suspected that this, more than affection, was the likely reason for the visit. Charlotte had an insatiable appetite for sweets and looked it, although her plump face was pretty, framed by her black hair.

The steps of the small wooden store were swept clean. The clapboards wore a new coat of whitewash. In the front window the geranium held onto one tiny pink bloom, the leaves a very deep green.

Mr. Tarantino spotted his granddaughter in the light that lingered in the doorway as they entered the store. "Bella! Bella! Carlotta!" It was easy to understand why Charlotte thought she was something special. She smiled as he walked over and embraced her, kissing her on both cheeks.

He remembered Molly even though she hadn't been in the store very often. "Signorina Molly!" he bellowed. "*Benvenuta!*" Mr. Tarantino had a way of making everyone seem important, so much so that she wanted to duck. "This is my cousin, Alfred."

"Alfredo," he nodded. "My pleasure."

In one narrow aisle just wide enough for one person, a colored woman was asking for red beans. "Ain't finding none, Mr. T."

"That's easy. Mr. Lonnie, he'll show you."

Lonnie sat on a stool near the counter. His blue-gray eyes seemed to float in their pink sockets. He smiled and stood up, tap-tapping his way down the aisle. He counted down a row of cans, then picked up the red beans. "*Fagioli* in can," he said in Mr. Tarantino's manner of speaking. He turned toward the woman with the beans in his outstretched hand.

"Mr. Lonnie, he holds in his head everything ina the store. You want peach. Mr. Lonnie gets you a peach." Mr. Tarantino went behind the counter, rang open the cash register and took the woman's money for the beans.

Molly guessed Mr. Lonnie made mistakes from time to time, maybe opening a can of soup to heat on the stove, only to discover it was something bad, like hominy or squash.

All of a sudden Mr. Tarantino began bellowing, "Punchinello, quite a fella!" He was almost an opera singer. "So Carlotta, you practice the dance? You also, Molly?"

"They make her play the piano," said Charlotte, sounding almost sympathetic.

"My favorite," said Mr. Lonnie. "I used to play myself." She knew that blind people sometimes played the piano quite well. Maybe *she* would play better when she was blind.

"Molly, you play the piano while Carlotta dance—you both gonna be famous as my *son!*" He seemed convinced that this was so and twirled his mustache in celebration. He handed each of them a Goo Goo Cluster.

"His *son* is a marionette," said Charlotte, biting into the candy. She seemed somewhat embarrassed that her grandfather would carry on so over a marionette. Her teeth became stuck together with the thick nougat. "You'll see," she managed to say.

Mr. Tarantino kept singing "Punchinello . . . quite a fella" and around the side of the counter tripped a marionette. He moved fluidly under the guidance of Mr. Tarantino's muscular forearms. Punchinello wore black and white harlequin pants, a red tie and purple pointy shoes. His green hat was tipped with a bell. Mr. Tarantino made him shake his head and jingle it. Molly watched Punchinello dance and sing his Italian songs, so taken with the magic of puppetry that soon she forgot he wasn't real . . . for Mr. Tarantino seemed to disappear, his voice now projected from the marionette's moving lips. She felt light and floaty. Punchinello took her into his world, so much so that she was startled when Charlotte tugged at her sleeve. Time was a messenger, Charlotte's stomach the receiver. "C'mon," she said. Molly followed Charlotte toward the rooms in back of the store where her grandparents lived.

Alfred stayed with Mr. Tarantino and Mr. Lonnie in the front of the store. He was also intrigued with Punchinello, but no more so than Mr. Lonnie who seemed to enjoy the show the same as if he could see it.

In the back, the kitchen was dimly lit by a small lamp glowing from the table. Chopped onions and green peppers were mounded on the cutting board. A flood of rich aromas watered her eyes. Basil, parsley, and nutmeg.

Mrs. Tarantino's apron was splattered with red, looking much like an artist's smock. She was round and very bossy. "Carlotta! *Avanti!*" She hugged Charlotte greedily and patted Molly on the back.

"*Salve!*" called Mrs. Angelo, Charlotte's great-grandmother. She waved one hand and kept stirring with the other. Molly thought the greeting meant either "hello" or "howdy." The two women, locked into Italian, made no attempt to get free.

Molly sat down beside Charlotte while Mrs. Tarantino dished up two bowls of ice cream. "*Spumone,*" she said. On the yellowed ceiling, shadows cast by the oil lamp circled within circles, each one snug inside the next. The two women talked heatedly— Molly was fairly certain it was about the red sauce they were cooking—but the words didn't sound like a real argument and soon she realized that their talk was an ingredient the same as oregano and garlic.

Mrs. Tarantino sat down and watched proudly as Charlotte

ate. She stroked her granddaughter's shiny hair. Charlotte leaned her head against her grandmother's shoulder, still spooning the ice cream. Mrs. Tarantino's eyes glowed as they followed the spoon. It seemed that at any moment she would take over and feed Charlotte. Instead she ruminated then spoke softly in Italian, her words flowing like a song. Molly recalled that most all of the musical terms were Italian. *Andante. Adagio. Alla misura.* Willie would say "Eye-talian." All at once Molly felt as she did every Saturday morning when the clock stopped, aware of an inner silence, weighted and dense, that would come just before she'd leave to catch the bus headed for Willie's. A big spoonful of the green spumone fell to her lap like a cold ball of hail. Never in her life would she be as welcome in a place as Charlotte was here.

PART TWO

Chapter SEVEN

From Crosstown Molly struggled with the overnight bag as she boarded the Madison Avenue bus. She knew Willie wouldn't be particularly happy to see her, especially not with the bag packed for spending the night with Byrd. Dropping a token into the slot, Molly felt conspicuous in her accordion-pleated skirt. Like a fan, the skirt opened and closed with her every movement. She imagined it playing "Lady of Spain." Lately, her mother spent the whole of every day sewing and had become engrossed with the precision of pleating. She followed each pattern exactly with no adjustments considered. The width of the pleats ranged from very large accordion down to tiny concertina. She had borrowed patterns, and, for the most part, they were in sizes too big for Molly, which meant she would have to wear the skirts forever. Always she hoped her mother was making them for someone else.

At night, and with equal enthusiasm, her mother put down the sewing in order to study about diseases spread by pigeons. As strange as that was, Molly wished that her mother would devote full time to her campaign to rid the city of pigeons, or just spend the day smoking like Ludie Finch—anything but the sewing. The bus started up before she found a seat. She bobbled from pole to pole hearing the "Beer Barrel Polka." She sat down, certain that the other passengers had been startled by the wailing discordancy of the flatted pleats. Somehow she knew that her mother's preoccupation was connected to—had risen out of— her loss of the baby.

There will be no baby had come in the quiet of morning when her parents talked in hushed voices. Now sadness rode like a filled water jar balanced precariously on top of her head, threatening to spill over. She wanted her mother's grief to stand before her—out from its hiding place.

The bus rumbled past the stores and houses. As she got closer to Willie's, dread thrummed inside her. Today she was supposed to know perfectly the "Spinning Song." All week she'd thought only of making the marionette, ignoring all else, and was ill prepared for Willie's scrutiny. On her lap the dark red music book looked the color of blood. Quickly she covered it with her tablet and tried again to sketch what was snagged and settling in her mind, a wide-eyed fellow with a half-moon smile and a round nose, wearing a straw hat and tap shoes. What with the bus stopping every few feet, then starting up abruptly, the dancer was awkwardly posed between a shuffle and a hop. A job for Lena, she thought, remembering her crisp drawings rendered so swiftly. The bus stopped sharply in front of her grandparents' house. Molly put the pencil in her purse and got off. The bus pulled away, blasting her with fumes. If Willie had stayed down on Bullfrog Corner where she belonged, Molly would be tap dancing with a marionette at this very moment.

Her grandparents' worn-out gingerbread house looked like a playhouse belonging to either the old Georgian home on one side or the huge old dilapidated boarding house on the other. She walked nervously across the street, along the crumbling walk, and up the hollow steps. Over her shoulder the stark dogwood branches reached like crooked fingers. She remembered the tree as it had looked in spring, dressed in green and splattered with white blossoms, each one in the shape of a cross. Sister Thomasina had said that each of the four petals was tipped with Jesus's blood because His cross was made of dogwood. Molly thought about telling this to Willie, but Willie already had a legend that said Jesus's cross was made of cypress, and she would probably consider Sister Thomasina's legend farfetched.

Her knot of concerns tightened as she walked across the porch planks. She set the overnight bag aside so that she'd not have to explain about spending the night with Byrd, and rang the doorbell. At once she was confronted by an odor so awful her head swooned and her eyes blurred.

Grandmother Willie never did much for Grandaddy Bob, but Molly knew that she was now in the kitchen making up for it by cooking brains and eggs, his favorite breakfast. The Hardys ate for the "starving Armenians" as well as for themselves, a habit carried forth from World War I. No doubt he was sitting back there patting his stomach and smacking loudly, satisfied that along with himself he was feeding his share of the hungry, all of this evidenced by the horrible smell. Because of his affection for brains, Molly could never really love Grandaddy Bob.

She heard the heavy shoes. Grandmother Willie stomped down the wide hall. "A gander of no good space," she called it, and now she was dodging the heap of plunder left in there—an old iron bed piled high with moth-eaten blankets, the porcelain bedpan used for the unspeakable necessities of illness, an old metal lamp that was cordless and bent, and the assortment of broken chairs. Her wending passage through the junkshop of hard memories was accomplished by a method not unlike braille, since the hall was a cold black cave and nobody was brave enough to screw a lightbulb into the frayed electrical cord dangling down from the middle of the ceiling like a hangman's noose. Willie closed the French doors—the air fighting back for a few seconds before surrendering—and now, after the pouf, she was crossing over the thin, exhausted Chinese rug in the living room. She tweaked the sheer curtain that was threadbare on the middle edge, and squinted through the door as if her glasses were underpowered. Molly adjusted her own glasses and focused her eyes.

Willie's hair was parted not exactly in the middle and was knotted in a bun stuck randomly with hair pins. Her olive skin wrinkled across her forehead and face. "You're just in time, Molly," she said as she opened the door. She was friendly now, but it wouldn't last.

"I already ate oatmeal," said Molly. It was a lie. She hadn't eaten oatmeal or anything else. Her mother hadn't been feeling well and had stayed in bed while her father attempted to cook breakfast. The oatmeal had looked okay until he flooded it with the thick cream. Molly could not swallow its richness so early in the morning. Her mother would trickle only a few droplets if at all, as though the beads of cream were rare. Her father savored each bite of his oatmeal soaked with cream and talked about his Mama Jo. "She spoiled me, angel," he said. Molly knew no one had spoiled her mother and she thought it was sort of a shame that no one had.

Willie pondered half a second before choosing to respond with relief at not having to cook more breakfast. This was a contrast to all the other old ladies Molly knew, especially Mrs. Flynn, Miss Doyle, and Godmother Byrd—all of them determined to feed you whether you were hungry or not. But for Willie, time spent cooking, sewing, or doing housework kept her from the Bible opened and waiting on the dining-room table *and* from teaching piano, both missions so strong she ignored the fact that the house was coming down around herself and Grandaddy Bob.

Years before, Grandmother Willie had told Grandaddy Bob that she wanted *off of* Bullfrog Corner in Horn Lake, Mississippi, and *into* Memphis, Tennessee. He had bowed to her wishes and packed up his family of five girls and the prized boy, and come up to rent the little house on Madison Avenue, later managing to scrape up enough money to buy it. Willie was after school. She wanted to teach, but first she had to go to school herself. She financed her education by writing articles for the *Progressive Farmer* concerning the domestic side of farm life. "A joke," her mother had said. "She still doesn't know a milk pail from a mop bucket." At times Molly was certain her mother and grandmother despised each other.

Grandmother Willie had taught math to high school students until she got too old. Now she pumped her granddaughters full of music and Bible. But Molly was certain that the Protestant cousins never considered themselves natives in the clutches of a zealous missionary. When Willie looked at her, most likely all she saw was a wild aborigine.

Inside the living room Molly looked at the portrait hanging on the wall and then at Willie, a thing she'd done before. Again she tried to see the resemblance between the young woman and the old. The young Willie with dark hair and a faint smile was pretty hanging above the shabby divan covered in fabric as scratchy as cut hay. Matching the features in the picture with the Willie standing before her was made impossible by the dowager's hump that gave the old woman the posture of a small camel as it pushed her neck and head forward. The word "dowager"—cousin to the rich—better suited Godmother Byrd than Willie. Byrd stood straight as an old queen, bearing without strain, it would seem, the royal emeralds and pearls.

"Come on back." Willie had lost her smile now, but it wasn't the smell of brains that had affected her. The truth was that she didn't seem to like these Saturday sessions any more than Molly did. "Your Grandaddy's just starting."

"I thought I'd just go and look at the *Angelus*," said Molly, stalling. She prayed mightily that the smell hadn't yet conquered the bedroom. She wasn't particularly interested in this painting, but no other works of art or entertainments hung on the walls in the direction *away* from the kitchen, although her wandering eye was searching frantically for a backup in case Willie thought the excuse a lame one.

She gave Molly her wondering look, the one with her lips

pursed as though drawn up with a drawstring. The dark questioning eyes were not quite hidden behind her glasses, which were smeared opaquely with what might have been glutinous stuff from the brains, the smell of them now invading Molly's nose with an odor so big she saw streaks of red and yellow.

Tireless, Grandmother Willie looked back and tried one more time. "I don't mind scrambling up an egg for you," she said. Molly pictured her wearing a chef's hat slanted forward and held in place by a chin strap. Didn't Willie know insincerity was a sin? It might not have been on the list, but some things you could just feel. "Oh, no thanks," she croaked, anxious for Willie to leave the room.

"Come back and see him anyhow," Willie insisted. "He has to be leaving soon. Got to get on down to the cows, you know."

"In just a minute." Wambling, Molly tugged at the sleeves of her brown wool sweater for something to hold onto. The edge of the left cuff was frayed the same as her nerves. She needed time to brace herself against the smell that was alive and growing in the air. The worst thing about it was that Grandaddy Bob was sitting back there in the kitchen eating what he had fed.

She remembered the brown and white faces of the cows, standing around as though they had all the time in the world, chewing grass and swishing tails and then licking the salt block with tongues as big as dogs' ears. And just when you'd be convinced they'd go on like this forever, Grandaddy Bob would appear with the feed and they'd all look up with their great brown eyes perky and bright, then moo a few times before kicking up dust in a wild stampede and, just before trampling him to death, skid to a stop not more than one foot in front of him. He never flinched, just stood there as still as the muddy water in the pond when the heifers weren't wading in it, the whole thing a matter of trust, one that had backfired on one of his old loyal cows.

After the feeding, Grandaddy would go and check the shoddy abandoned house on Bullfrog Corner, although the only thing to check was whether or not it had fallen down. The house wasn't much good for anything, except offering shelter for the plague of wasps living in there, but he sometimes dried peanut vines on the tin roof so hot they roasted right there on the spot.

In Willie's bedroom, the farm people in the painting had heard the tolling of church bells and were praying the Angelus. The painting was dark and you couldn't really tell if it was morning or evening. Odd that Willie owned such a painting, since the devotion was Catholic.

Below the *Angelus* was the small fireplace where her mother would have huddled as a girl with the rest of the Hardy family, the uncertain faces smudged with black from the coal held in their hands. Each child would place one piece at a time on the grate, then—and for each piece thereafter—the whole family would sing a hymn of gratitude to God Almighty for providing the warmth.

Willie had been a Methodist, but love for the Bible and the evangelism of the Reverend Billy Graham had merged to light a holy path that led her straight to the Baptist Church. She was then "submerged" in what Molly figured must have been a really big baptismal font. She imagined Willie wearing a white-skirted bathing suit gathered at the waist like an apron, and around her neck, a circle of pink bubbles that reflected both the rapture in the faces of the church members who looked on and her own face radiant beneath a white bathing cap.

Willie couldn't swim and was no doubt terrified of the vat of water, but with her sort of commitment, she most likely thought that Jesus Himself was dunking her and that had kept her calm.

Grandaddy Bob had shown no concern when she converted. Years ago, in a rare sentence that had contained more than five words, he announced emphatically that the Methodists were hypocrites—"I'll not be goin' to church ever again."

Light beamed in on Willie's nubby green and yellow bedspread like sun on a field of ripe corn. Hers was the only warm room in the house. Grandaddy Bob's room was cold, the old bathroom next to it colder still. Fear of whatever lived under the claw-foot tub that stood on the worn speckled linoleum kept Molly from going in there no matter what the emergency. She had known what to expect of the snakes that had lived in her own room—they had made no opportunities, had taken no chances—whereas the something she couldn't see under the tub in Grandaddy Bob's bathroom might crawl out when disturbed by running water in the sink or flushing the commode. Visiting the Hardy house was unhealthy at best.

Grandaddy Bob and Willie had separate rooms, yet somehow they'd gotten together enough times to have produced six children. The only other bedroom had been occupied by "Aunty," Grandaddy's ancient aunt, long since dead, so most likely the children had slept in the cold dark hall. Molly pictured all six of them lined up on cots according to age and covered with thin blankets—her mother third from the end. Aunty in her yellowed lace cap peeked in on them from the middle bedroom, a black woolen shawl embroidered with pink roses snugged around her slight shoulders, carrying a lantern glowing a faint red. When she was very young, Molly had caught sight of Aunty just long enough to hold her in a memory that was now as frail as she had been.

As long as somebody remembered, the dead were still sort of alive and so was Aunty. Someday Molly would be solely responsible for her memory. And after she herself was gone, Aunty would be too.

Because of nagging lists of venial sins that kept the dead from resting in peace, most of them could not just *be dead* anyhow. Ghosts milled around in daytime, prowled at night. That explained many of the noises in her own house as well as certain odors and the movements of air. Suspended in time, these spirits were the grays—the not-altogether-bad-or-good-dead— hanging around in a purgatorial fog, praying mightily for the pure light of Heaven.

She thought the people in the *Angelus* were praying to get off the farm like Willie had done. Still, looking around the old house, Molly wondered if the Hardys were all that much better off in the city.

"Molly," called Grandmother Willie. Her voice was a tolling bell. Molly took one last breath of clean air and cut through the thick atmosphere of the living room. She met the rankness of the dining room and at the cusp of the kitchen struggled to enter, but could only nod at Grandaddy Bob from the doorway. Here the brain air was thoroughly stout.

"Morning, Molly," he said, moving a forkful of gray matter toward his round pink face. She closed her eyes for a second, delirious and unable to watch his mouth. He was oblivious of the smell, almost cheerful. On his plate the eggs were two yellow eyes looking up at him from either side of the big nose of brains. "Have some breakfast?" he asked.

She would have to answer. The breath she was holding filled up her lungs like a hot-air balloon. She felt herself rise slightly. To stay on the ground she let out little bleats of air. His food was getting cold as he patiently waited for her answer. She wanted to say she was truly sorry, but talking would require opening her mouth and that meant the air touching the brains would then be inside her.

She spit out "No, thanks," then waved, fleeing to the dining room where she sat down hard on the piano bench, the bump an attempt at shooting the smell back out of her nose. She played "Onward Christian Soldiers" to entertain him.

But her playing was tentative and not so much a march as a stroll. Soon Willie came in and took over. "You rest a minute," she said. With her old gnarled fingers, the stomping hymn was enhanced with runs, trills, and grace notes, the veins in her hands turning a very dark blue with blood steadily pumping the rhythm that surely matched the vibrant beat of her heart . . . and also Molly's, though inside herself she tried hard to deny it. When Willie really got going and played louder, the room filled up with Baptist soldiers dressed in very plain navy blue suits and dresses, carrying white Bibles in their hands and fire in their hearts. Then it was—but only for a moment when she felt herself almost marching in step with them—that Molly considered changing religions.

No such temptation ever rose when *she* played the hymn. Willie got up and motioned for Molly to sit down.

Grandaddy scraped the chair away from the kitchen table, came into the dining room, and picked his old brown rain-beaten hat off of the top of the piano where it rested beside the five porcelain French peasants he'd collected for Willie, odd since she had no appreciation for such things. He called them his "little girls." "This one's your mother, Molly," he said as he touched the petite waif with a black kerchief tied under her chin. Leaving the room, he waved his arm back and forth as limply as a cow swishing its tail. His "'Bye" stretched out long and smooth, then lipped a little before the sound faded. He walked out the door, shambled down the steps and started up his dusty black car, the old motor grinding.

The brain odor seemed to leave with him; still, Molly was more comfortable in the house when Grandaddy was in it. Willie pulled up her chair. She hoped her grandmother wouldn't decide to move over and sit on the bench beside her. If she sat that close, all the air would drain from the room.

Willie turned to the "Spinning Song." "You might want it for recital," she hinted.

"I could play the 'Minuet in G,'" said Molly, not wanting to get stuck with the monotonous spinning wheel.

"I've committed it to your cousin Marsha," she said.

She always got firsts. There was nothing new about that. In a white dress Marsha looked like a marshmallow. The "Minuet in G" was a marshmallow sort of tune and Molly was sick of it anyhow.

Molly turned to the page that pictured the Italian people dancing, holding hands and kicking up their heels. She almost laughed thinking how she could accompany herself on the red skirt pleated every quarter inch like a concertina. Then she remembered that Willie didn't believe in dancing and wished the music publishers had left off the illustration. She swallowed and said, "I thought maybe I could play the 'Tarantella' for the recital."

"It just seems a little wild, Molly," she said, emphasizing the *wild* as if all Italians were. Charlotte's grandfather, Mr. Tarantino, got a little excited once in a while, but the sound was not so much wild as it was happy. The only things wild about Mrs. Tarantino and Mrs. Angelo were the spices they shook into their vat of spaghetti.

Wild was what Willie thought about her father. Neither side of the family was happy when he and her mother married. "Your Aunts Emalene, Willene, Jesse, and Ella W.—so horrible a name she wouldn't let anyone say it—quacked like a brace of ducks," her father had said. "Uncle Bob Roy hiccupped the whole way. Like an old drake." When he had finished mimicking the Hardys, he focused his attention on his own sisters. "Aunt Rose Kate, Aunt Kathleen, and Aunt Nellie honked into their Irish lace handkerchiefs like a gaggle of geese. What a show."

Molly always pictured the geese and ducks waddling around

the edge of a small pond, all of them afraid to drink or swim in the same water.

After setting the metronome, Willie got up and began sorting through the biblical figures piled on the dining room table, ready to act out the old stories. The flannel board stood upright and opened. Moses and Noah, both with white beards, lay on either side of the Ark of the Covenant that glistened like gold in the gray shadows of the room. Sampson was taller than the patriarchs, Goliath taller still. Delilah was sexy, the other women dowdy. All week Molly had been bombarded with the *Baltimore Catechism* questions as well as stories from *Lives of Saints*. Now, just as she was recovering, the Bible characters were lined up in a procession, wearing their best robes and waiting to go on stage.

Molly played the "Spinning Song," feeling herself go around and around as her fingers worked the simple pattern of notes over and over again, until finally she was playing the song and thinking about something else at the same time. Her mother had worn a plain dark suit for the wedding. Probably she'd had no money for a white gown. Molly worried over such plainness on their wedding day.

The Hardy family was too big to fit into one car, so they'd made two trips to the church rectory, but the priest, anxious to get it over with, had performed the ceremony in between the first and second shifts with only half of the Hardys witnessing her mother's downfall. Willie had made the first shift.

"Too fast, Molly," said Willie. "I can't hear the notes. Don't you be using the pedal. Are you?"

"No, ma'am," she said. She wasn't really sure. She wanted to please her and was earnestly spinning now. Clackety-clack, clackety-clack. The work was tedious, the strain unnatural in its slowness. While her left hand continued to play, she reached up with the right one and quickly set the metronome ticking about the same speed as the human heart. To keep the wheel running smoothly she began pressing the pedal and letting off . . . going hard at it, dizzily spinning spinning, round and round. The room filled up with dazzling white. She kept pressing the pedal, letting off before Willie could see, the metronome ticking like a time bomb, the proliferation of yarn piled to the ceiling. The wool of lambs. She imagined Willie weaving a big white cloth of salvation, then wrapping her from head to toe like a mummy.

Molly was into the hundredth skein. The yarn, spun with deliberation and fortitude, suddenly turned orange when Willie's voice broke in. Her eyes were hard.

"You're just a pounding it out, Molly. *Listen*. Listen to yourself!" The lines on her grandmother's face were now deep crevices and she felt herself starting to fall into one of them. She wanted to close the music book and leave the room.

"The metronome seems to have inched up maybe a notch or two." Molly knew what came next and slumped her shoulders. She was mightily tired even before she heard the words. "On slow."

"I promise to slow *down*," said Molly, wanting a second chance. The yarn had changed to violet.

There was no room for forgiveness. Willie set the metronome

on "drag-ass," as Nat would say when no one was around. Now Molly's wheel would be the slowest one in the world, her yarn thin, scraggly, and worst of all, beige. She heard herself moan. Willie looked puzzled, unsure of where the sound came from.

The single-mindedness of the metronome steadily ticked in her ears and for a while Molly concentrated on the music and nothing else, ponderously focusing her eyes on each bar. But Willie was not satisfied with the performance.

"You've been practicing with the mandolin attachment again, haven't you?" she accused. Molly's silence owned up to it, while inside herself she held dear the apparatus that changed the keyboard from ordinary to *wow*!

Willie stood firm on her notion that Molly's piano had come straight out of a dance hall. "Colors the melody in such ways as God *nor* Mozart never intended," she said.

Did it ever. With the flip of a bar, the music went to another time and place, and then—with the tinkling mandolin tunes pouring from her fingers—she was a musician in Italy or some other foreign place—always at night—and the tinny sound serenaded a slice of moon so beautiful that anyone looking up would feel glad. The moon was the rarest thing, maybe the light of the Holy Ghost.

Finally they broke for the Bible. "I want you to do the statue of gold today." She was pointing at the stack of figures, the big Nebuchadnezzar on top. Instead of the parting of the Red Sea or Noah's ark—the sort of stories she saved for the cousins— Willie was forever insisting that Molly ponder the passages about idols. Most likely she held that statues of the Blessed

Mother and the other saints standing on pedestals in Catholic Churches were attended by crowds of idolators, one of them Molly.

Confirming Willie's suspicion that she was headed for hell, Molly now disgraced herself by forgetting who in blazes Nebuchadnezzar *was*. "I can't think who," she said, her mind a blank slate. Even worse, she was seeing two of him.

Willie wiped the fog off her glasses with her apron, and finding patience, told the story herself. Raising both shoulders, her voice quivered with excitement as she let loose Daniel. As the story unfolded she placed the characters on the flannel board. Her narration was as dramatic as adding sound to a silent movie.

Thou, O king, hast made a decree, that every man that shall hear the sound of the cornet, flute, harp, sackbut, psaltery, dulcimer, and all kinds of musick, shall fall down and worship the golden image: And whoso falleth not down and worshippeth, *that* he should be cast into the midst of a burning fiery furnace.

Inspired by the list of the instruments, Molly thought of "Macnamara's Band," her father's favorite record. He would turn it up real loud and march around the house singing. He'd get Lena and Molly and sometimes her mother, singing along. Even Nat would put down his Booth Tarkington or whatever book he was reading and join in when he heard the two pot tops clash together like cymbals.

Again Willie listed the instruments so that Molly would never again forget, adding some that the Bible never mentioned—banjos and a glockenspiel. And then Molly heard "Alexander's Ragtime Band" playing in her head and imagined herself marching in step with musicians carrying instruments polished to a blinding shine and herself wearing a white majorette costume, a tall hat circled in a red band and boots with tassels that flapped. She was twirling a baton.

Willie's voice took on depth as she congratulated Shadrach, Meshach, and Abednego for resisting the worship of the big golden idol, the message delivered as subtly as a gust of air blown from a tuba. Molly's head was wildly playing the whatchamacallit of John Philip Sousa.

She felt herself glowing all over. Willie saw the sign and mistook it for rapture over the Word. Triumphantly she issued the entreaty: "Why not spend the night?"

Superior peripheral vision was a strength that sometimes made up for her eye that wandered. Willie's eyes were now looking directly at her left cheek. Hastily she took up with the "Spinning Song" as though she'd not heard the crackling voice of her grandmother nor felt the sting of her stare.

"The early service. We'll go then," said Willie, louder now than God.

There it was, Willie's mecca—Bellvue Baptist Church—out in the open and reaching, and Molly with no place to hide. She shriveled up, pressing elbows into her ribcage. "Going there would be a mortal sin!"

The words struck Willie's ears—she winced, but held back and said nothing. She began fidgeting with the color crayons, dumping them out on the table. Her chest heaved. Without ever showing a flame she was dangerously hot. Combustible. And it was Molly's own fault. She'd encouraged Willie in the first place by selecting "Onward Christian Soldiers" when she should have played the painful "Dies Irae," scaring her off with its mysterious Latin undertone. When you sang the "Dies Irae" you could hear the hollow voices of the ghosts singing with you, holding onto the airy ringing notes longer because they needed no breath. When you stopped for a minute, you'd catch them at it—the moaning of black centuries that pulled time back into itself. Then, for a second, you'd see them lined up in the pews, wearing brown hooded robes and carrying white candles, the smoke of yellow flames drifting from the ancient past.

But Molly would never mention the invitations to Bellvue to her mother or father, no matter how hard Willie backed her against the wall. At the same time, she was not going to tell Willie that she was spending the night with Godmother Byrd.

Willie said, "You never finished up with your colors. Joseph's brothers haven't been done yet except for the hair and why did you make it red? I don't think they would've had red."

Somehow Molly accepted that she must come back the next Saturday and the many Saturdays that followed—right up until the recital—but right now she was going to give the brothers orange and purple robes, and very deep blue eyes with red brows and lashes. Then she said it and she didn't know why she said it. "Mother lost the baby. . . ." The wholeness of the words was why she had to say them. Now they had been set free from silence, and she thought of the baby in a bubble that had just popped in the air. And now the baby was floating in space.

"You know about it, then." Willie paused before saying anything else. "She was some too old for having another one. The Lord knows what He's doing. You can be sure of that." In truth it seemed that she was glad the baby wasn't going to be around—that she wouldn't have another idolater to worry over. "Elizabeth was downright obsessed on having it. Just set stubborn for it."

Then, having separated the wheat from the chaff, she sat down. And for a while she sucked her nail and pondered, her black eyes stilled and glossy as if painted on her face. "How is Elizabeth?"

"She mostly sews," said Molly. Her hands were pushing and pulling the sides of her skirt as if by reflex. "And she's going to get rid of all the pigeons."

"Always one for extremes," said Willie. "Always has been."

Molly didn't care about extremes. And right now she didn't care to think about her mother and sewing and the pigeons, or the Bible or music. None of it. She only wanted to know whether or not Grandmother Willie believed in Limbo.

Chapter EIGHT

"I want Elizabeth to have some seeds." Willie drew Molly away from the piano, out of the dining room and into the kitchen. The porcelain sink was big as a bathtub and full of dirty dishes. Willie picked a few small jars from the window sill. The hazy old glass windowpanes bubbled and waved like water. Willie had something on her mind as she put the jars in a brown paper sack. Her forehead was knotted with ideas.

The screened back porch was covered with old latticework. Bright diamonds of sunlight shown through the spaces. The porch itself smelled musty, and the walls were streaked with mildew behind the tools—the posthole digger, the rake, and the hoe—all propped in the corner, rusting. Willie picked up the old cultivator. "The iris need culling," she said. "Some are big as sweet potatoes." From behind the Mother Hubbard washboard, she pulled out a croaker sack good for fifty pounds.

"I don't think I could carry it on the bus, Grandmother."

"Oh, I hadn't thought," she said, letting the cultivator fall with a clang. Like most everything in the house, the proper place for it was wherever it landed. "Next time you come in the car, then."

She gave the Flanagans iris every year. And always they would plant them. After a season, when the tubers had grown fat and had multiplied, they would have to be dug up, separated and replanted. Each year the iris beds grew larger and always there were extras. Then Molly was sent up and down the street with a peck of tubers piled high in the wheelbarrow for sharing with the neighbors, unusual since her mother rarely gave things away. Her father would ask that her mother not accept any more iris tubers. He saw that the planting, digging up, and planting again was as monotonous as a wheel traveling in a circle. "Rhizomes," she'd say without looking at him, "they're called *rhizomes*." And he wouldn't mention it again until the next year.

Molly thought her mother just couldn't say no to Willie, and that she would go on accepting the unwanted iris until Willie died. After that, the distribution of tubers would continue with her mother at the helm, and since they would be obligated to dig up all of Willie's untended iris and plant them, the yield would increase tenfold until the entire backyard was under cultivation the same as in the pictures of the Victory Garden. With the great lot of tubers and no place to plant them, Molly would then be required to push the wheelbarrow up and down not only Theola—except for the Finches' she couldn't think of a yard left on Theola Avenue that didn't already have a thick patch of iris—but also Tutwiler, Claybrook, Faxon, and on and on. Surely Alfred would help—she could count on Alfred—until the heart of Memphis in springtime was blooming with purple, white, yellow, gold, brown, and pink flags waving hope. And then people from all over the South—the whole country, maybe even the world—would come and see the iris and they would say that Memphis was just about the same as Holland. From heaven—Molly was certain her grandmother would go there—

Willie would be knocked out over Elizabeth Flanagan's accom-
plishment and Molly herself would own a share of the credit.

Her mother and grandmother never talked much and maybe
the iris was the only thing holding them together, but even so,
Willie's doling out of tubers was getting plenty old. Trans-
portation by car probably would not happen until the recital,
so maybe Molly had just avoided the annual relocation of the
iris altogether. By then the cold weather might well scoot any
immediate need of culling the iris tubers right out of Willie's
head.

They stepped out on the wooden stoop and, for a moment,
Willie looked at the sky and then all around the little yard. Her
busy eyes raced from the rose bush to the top of the big oak tree
and on to the sunflower stalks drooping in the alley, the seeds
pilfered in late summer by the cardinals who had beat her to it.
With her hoe she drubbed at the weeds that separated the pan-
icles of dried flowers in her old rough garden. She was adamant
that Jesus would soon come, but had said she wasn't sure what
form He would take. Often when she'd search the yard, shaking
the branches of each bush and peering at each leaf and insect
through her magnifying glass, her fear of missing Him disguised
as nature was apparent.

In the garden patch Molly could hardly tell the flowers from
the weeds. Willie had no problem and pointed at the clumps of
nasturtiums, zinnias, and the datura that she called "angel's
trumpet." She pinched heads off the bachelor's buttons and said,
"Once you get these started—blue, you see the color, now don't
you—you won't ever get rid of them." She said it as if these

flowers, like Molly, were just something to put up with. The bachelor's buttons *were* faintly blue, just like she said.

What if her mother didn't like bachelor's buttons? Would she plant them anyhow? She pressed the crisp heads into one of the jars and closed the lid before Willie could hand her more. "This one's full," Molly said.

Seed gathering came natural to this family. Her mother—at great risk to her reputation—had pinched dried thyme from Monticello, a spent daisy from the Hermitage and a sprig of sage from Mt. Vernon. Later she shared the seeds and dried herbs with Willie. Each time Willie looked keenly at the gifts as if she suspected theft, but accepted the seeds and herbs anyhow, no questions asked.

"Here's Joseph's coat." She delighted in the stiff red flowers still half-alive in spite of being dried by the sun and chilled by fall nights. "They grow real thick," she said, separating the seeds with her old blue fingers. "They like sun. Be sure to plant them in sun. But not too much water. Damping off of seeds comes when you give too much."

Willie loaded her down with the spent heads of snapdragons and sweet peas. Her mother would have to figure out someplace to plant all these seeds. At the insistence of Molly's father, four o'clocks crowded her sunniest flower bed, taking over in summer just after the iris were clipped back in the shape of fans. The four o'clocks opened at the correct hour like the mouths of baby birds. Molly thought the flowers might make her mother sad now.

Willie was busily stacking the seed jars in the sack. There

seemed to be no end to it. Molly said, "I think it's time for me to catch the bus." Before Willie could say otherwise, she went inside, picked up the music book from the piano, retrieved the overnight bag from the porch, and ran out to the backyard again. Motioning toward the alley, she said, "I'll just go on out the back way."

"The back way?" Never before had it occurred to Willie that another way out existed, the surprise a little like Alfred's discovery that while two and two make four, the sum was the same when adding three plus one. Willie didn't seem to notice the overnight bag.

As Molly opened the gate to the alley, Willie gave up and in a resigned voice said, "Go ahead, then . . . with the 'Tarantella,' I mean. I guess it's as good as any." In truth she didn't seem to believe it. She was shaking her head.

Not wanting to give Willie time to change her mind, Molly swung through the gate and into the alley, where she began kicking rocks, taking long strides and feeling free. Still it was no good. The lesson had gone badly, the Bible story yet worse, and now and on top of it all, the half-hearted permission to actually play her own selection tainted the music. She felt in her pocket for her token and discovered that it was gone. She glanced back at Willie who was minding her dead flowers like a caretaker in a neglected cemetery. Rather than ask her for money, Molly quickly walked away.

Chapter NINE

On Tucker Street, she walked by Foppiano's grocery. It was two stories high on a street of one-storied houses. She thought that buildings in Italy would look like that, stuccoed with tin roofs. An RC Cola decal was stuck on the door. And in the window a sign said "Go Get a Goo Goo . . . It's Good," the same as Tarantino's. Mr. Tarantino would say, "In America you all stuck together with *il dolciume*. What's a Goo Goo? That'sa bambino talk." He would make a smacking sound and ring up the cash register, smiling. Maybe immigrating from Italy to Memphis wasn't as difficult as coming on up from Mississippi.

The Tarantinos approved of Charlotte even when she bungled the steps of her latest tap dance. On the other hand, they'd not seen the short royal blue satin costume she wore for the "Take Me Out to the Ballgame" routine. If they did, Molly was certain they'd say something about it, in Italian. The Tarantinos would hardly approve of bare arms and legs, no matter how much they loved America, and Charlotte.

Molly crossed Poplar Avenue and focused her eyes by squinting at the statue of Mayor E. H. Crump standing at the entrance to Overton Park. It was said that Mr. Crump had ruled over Memphis for more than forty years and that he still ran things from the grave. Her father said that Boss Crump had put the Flanagans out of business; Grandmother Willie said he took his sweet time about doing it.

Molly entered the park, a great forest in the middle of town. In the clearings stood the landmarks of Memphis: Brooks Art Gallery, the zoo, the Shell, the Doughboy erected in honor of the soldiers who served in World War I, and the Rose Garden that grew on the site of the old Japanese Garden—which had been torn down after Pearl Harbor.

As she passed the gallery she was thinking that *Jesus in Agony in the Garden* might look somewhat better hanging up high on one of the big walls in there. Someday her father might let them have it. She'd replace it with one of Lena's drawings. Her work was irresistible, like hope.

Molly came to the Shell where outdoor concerts and plays were held in summer. The music was the grandest thing, especially when a slight breeze chased the humidity, but still grand even when sweat poured inside your shirt. At the end of summer Nat had starred in the play. The drama critic for the newspaper had insinuated that the escape of the python had been a hoax created to attract attention to the performance. Nat had gone along with it, saying that the python had won a supporting role as the creature of legend. The snake did not appear opening night, but Nat gave the performance of his life, winning a long round of applause and the great admiration of their parents, friends, and relatives.

Molly sat on a bench in the last row and looked down at the giant shell arched above the stage. It was faintly pink with a rainbow painted inside. She imagined herself standing nervously in the wings wearing a dress of coral taffeta, waiting for the conductor's signal. He nodded and then she walked gracefully toward the piano. She sat down, lightly lifting her hands, resting them in her lap, then raised them to the playing position. The maestro tapped his baton and she began. She played the first part of the "Tarantella" lively and fast and moderately loud. The melody was simple and pure. The violins and cellos accompanied her for the counter melody that softened before gradually leading to *sforzando* when the whole orchestra joined in, then soft again before climbing to a crescendo. She was repeating the whole of it when the hairy tarantula crawled out from nowhere and bit her on the arm. Then she played furiously and loud and long—again and again—to prevent herself from falling into a coma and yielding to its deadly poison. Her head whirled as she hammered the keys wildly, the swelling of music filling the whole outdoors, so great the outflow, the purge of her energy, that not only did she *live* but the magnificence of her music moved the audience to their feet! And when she rose and curtsied, the roar of applause rang in her head.

The concert ended when a tractor cranked and started cutting grass nearby, drowning out her thunder. In truth she wondered if her father and mother and Nat would all come to her recital. And if she made mistakes, would they still clap?

The seed jars rattled as she walked toward the zoo. A few children were splashing in the wading pool that she'd never been allowed to play in as a small child because other children peed in it. Across a wide playing field, Rainbow Lake sparkled in the sun.

Exotic bird calls and the chattering of monkeys pecked at the stillness. She did not enter the zoo, but looked through the fence as she walked alongside it. A peacock picked his way across the dry grass, his brilliant blue-and-green tail feathers folded modestly. A hyena laughed hysterically. The zoo looked almost empty of people, but slouched against the fence rail of the pony ride, the carny boy was watching her as she passed. She hugged the brown sack close to her chest and kept walking. Lately, each time she went to the zoo, he was always there. He stared at her as he unbuckled a small saddle from a brown pony and continued to stare even as he ambled over to the rack and hung it up. She looked straight ahead, but in the corner of her eye saw him filling the trough with water. Still watching her. She walked down Galloway and away from him.

Ahead of her, through the trees, she could see the top of the Conservatory, a building four stories high, with the finest teachers in Memphis. And it was there that Byrd wanted to send her to study music. Molly knew it wouldn't happen. Willie was not likely to relinquish her role as teacher until Molly became a Baptist. But the real reason she'd never go, and she knew it very well, was that there was little hope she'd ever be accepted. If she were, she knew the best pianists were assigned to the large airy rooms on the first floor; those with lesser talent climbed the stairway to their places above—assigned according to ability, or the lack of it. If by chance she was ever accepted, no doubt she'd have to play an out-of-tune piano in an isolated corner of the fifth-floor attic.

High noon and her hair was hot and dripping wet in the heat.

Turning the corner, she began walking fast, as she was almost to Byrd's.

Suddenly Molly realized how close Byrd's house was to Willie's. Distance in miles wasn't the only way of measuring things, she thought. Slowly the sun would move through the afternoon toward the river, allowing the long shadows of fall to creep coolly over the city. Her father had said that the feet of Memphis were stuck firmly in the muddy banks of the Mississippi and that the body grew eastward. If that was so, then the Flanagans' house was in the belly; Byrd's and Willie's, the heart and mind.

And she knew that the city—the whole world for that matter—was far below Heaven or even Purgatory—somewhere south of Limbo, but way north of Hell.

Rounding the corner she passed under the old elms standing like sentries along the narrow parkway. Tree shadows blackened the hill-yards that grew from the sidewalk like ancient mounds. Her father had said that hills in Memphis were significant, because anything that rises above the flat terrain offers a rare view of things. She found herself wondering if Byrd might accept some of Willie's seeds—snapdragons or bachelor's buttons, or zinnias. But Byrd's yard was deep in shade and covered with ivy. Molly tucked the sack of jars under a cascading vine on the retaining wall and left it there. Later, like her mother, she'd take the seeds home whether she wanted them or not.

Molly looked down the street, where the hill tapered to a flat, where that certain house with secret Mediterranean windows, haunted balconies, and shaded passageways seemed like a sepulchre. Long ago a little boy had drowned there in the basement swimming pool. She could not remember the boy's age, but she knew that things appeared larger under water so if he had been three, he might have looked five on the bottom of the pool—almost as if he'd lived two years more. She wondered if Limbo was like that—like floating in water. She wiped her forehead and determined not to think of it again.

Chapter TEN

Molly's eyes followed the seventeen steps dividing the sea of ivy that climbed toward her Godmother Byrd's dark brick bungalow. Byrd rested on the wicker sofa on the porch, almost hidden by a wall of ligustrum. She rose to greet Molly, her stout figure moving slowly toward the door where she stood like a portrait under the arch. "Molly, I'm here . . . on the porch." An ecru jabot with tatted edging was held to her brown crepe dress by the diamond bar pin that she always wore. Her white hair curled gently round her soft face.

"I'm coming, Byrd."

The twelfth step widened to a landing where a birdbath sprouted like a tulip on the spread of concrete. Molly had never seen any birds bathing in it.

"Why don't the birds ever go in their bath?" she called.

"It's too much trouble to put water in it, dear." Byrd's voice shone down from above, her expression patient and solemn as an old saint. From the phonograph, a crystal voice sang "Ave Maria."

When Molly reached the porch Byrd hugged her. "Come on in, dear," she said. Her great bosom was soft as a feather pillow. She held Molly's hand with short plump fingers that shone with diamonds in platinum settings. She smelled of lilac.

Inside the shadows blended with the dark gum woodwork and heavy walnut furniture. Fat chairs were covered in tapestries of maroon and brown. Above the fireplace hung the painting of a cathedral, its spires coddled by thin clouds. Old lace draped the windows, falling as soft folds against the dark floor.

Only Byrd's bright green parrot, Hi Boy, animated the gloom. As far as Molly knew, Hi Boy had never left his cage since the day of his arrival, how long ago?

"How old is Hi Boy, Byrd?" His eyes looked wary and intent.

"Dear, you do ask questions. I'm not really sure. My John— may his soul rest in peace—bought him when we traveled around the world." Byrd pressed her white curls into place. "Hi Boy was very old even then. Surely he has the wisdom of the ages, as far as birds are concerned."

She pictured Byrd on an ocean liner holding the cage, a breeze blowing her hair. She wondered if it was white then. Grandmother Willie had never traveled farther than Bullfrog Corner.

The grandfather clock gonged four times. Hi Boy rustled his feathers and squawked. "Twelve o'clock. All is well. All is well."

Molly looked at the clock. "But it's only four."

Byrd laughed. "John got the old bird talking back to the clock for sure, but never could he get him counting properly. It's always twelve o'clock to Hi Boy. He's not quite so wise after all."

Hi Boy shed wisdom the same as he did feathers. Something that could clearly be seen. Molly shrugged, feeling stiff and helpless, like time was standing still. If both her parents died, then Byrd would be responsible for her religious upbringing. She would then probably come to live here.

"Honestly, you seem to have grown this week," said Byrd. "And speaking of time. Where has it gone? Your birthday's next month. And then a piano recital?"

"Yes, ma'am. The first week in December." She was wholly glad for the lot of time between then and now, but suddenly felt that it wasn't enough. "It's just my cousins on Mother's side—and me. Grandmother Willie teaches us all."

"Oh, yes. Your Grandmother Willie." Byrd smiled reluctantly, the corners of her mouth curving upward in a fix. "Someday you'll play at the Conservatory. But your grandmother's remarkable to have the ability to teach you . . . and the patience."

Molly thought it was kind of Byrd to say something nice about Willie. She could not recall Willie saying anything at all about Byrd. "You could come to the recital if you wanted." She didn't know why she'd said it. She knew it wasn't so. The two sides of her family never mixed.

"Hardly possible," said Byrd. "I keep to my boundaries. Always we must restrain ourselves." Her voice had raised in what seemed a warning that Willie's influence might lead Molly onto a path of righteousness different from their own, and that she might get lost out there. But Willie hadn't given her a King James like the ones she'd given the cousins. Their Bibles were white. The black Douay Rheims was proof that Willie was still mad at her mother for marrying her father. Molly wondered how it might be without any religion at all.

Byrd glanced at Molly's music book still tucked under her arm. She opened the piano, a resigned expression on her face.

"I never learned to play, but I can listen. Why not practice your recital piece?"

Molly pulled out the bench and sat down. She wanted to tell Byrd that Grandmother Willie never played what she *taught*— that she never struggled with Mozart and Bach, that her gnarled fingers paid no attention to *pocos* or *bravissimos*, and that she used the forbidden pedal to connect the rolling chords of "Onward Christian Soldiers" and to swell its stomping rhythm. But she stayed silent, warming up with the scales instead. Reluctantly, Byrd switched off the "Ave Maria."

Molly did not yet know "Tarantella" well enough to play it for Byrd, but instead of explaining that the recital piece had only just been assigned, she made her way through the "Minuet in G." She made only a few mistakes. Only then, at the end of the piece, did Byrd's face relax.

"Keep on, dear. I'll bring some lemonade. There's hope for the Conservatory."

Molly's fingers again wandered through the minuet. She was playing it a third time when Byrd brought the lemonade in a crystal glass, the cubes of ice tinkling. The glass shone in the waxed wood as she set it down on a silver coaster.

"Very good, dear. I'll be out on the porch, listening." She walked heavily across the floor and out the door. Hi Boy preened his feathers. Molly played for a few seconds without looking at her fingers, but felt unsure of whether or not she could do so at length, and Willie would insist for the recital. She paused, glancing at the lemonade. Hi Boy made a clacking sound in his throat.

She remembered how Jane had interrupted her practice at home a few days before—only she hadn't brought lemonade. Jane had barged right in the house without knocking, catching her breath as if she'd been chased. She had taken over the piano, singing and playing in an odd way that was both sweet and bitter, singing so softly that only Molly could hear.

"There's a place in France where women wear no pants." Jane had sung it over and over, whispering that someday she would dance like Gypsy Rose Lee and take off all her clothes on stage. One garment at a time. The tears in her eyes glistened but never fell.

Molly had listened hard, then felt a stirring inside like an elevator coming down too fast. She was confused, but instead of asking what or why, she had run to the kitchen window to make sure her mother had not heard, that she was still in the backyard pruning the roses.

Now Molly pressed the keys lightly; her face felt warm as Jane's song crept out. Byrd wouldn't approve of such a song any more than Grandmother Willie, but Willie would not be surprised to hear a Catholic sing it. She imagined the startled expressions on the faces of the audience at the recital if suddenly she should play it.

"I can't hear you, dear," called Byrd.

Again Molly worried that Nat was somehow responsible for Jane's knowing about sex. She stared at Beethoven's notes and turned the page, her fingers stiffening. She played more loudly.

Byrd rocked on the porch, the runners of the chair as steady as a metronome. Molly played faster than Byrd rocked.

"Better slow down a bit, dear," said Byrd. "In Beethoven's day, the ladies made coquettish swirls when they danced the minuet. Give them a little more time."

Molly played it again, but slower. The dancers would barely be moving now. If Willie realized that the minuet was a dance, would she then tear it from the music book?

Molly grew tired and Byrd seemed to understand. Or maybe she was tired, too. "That should be enough for today, dear."

Molly shook her hands just as Grandmother Willie had taught to relieve the cramped fingers. She was thankful for the end of practice. Willie would have made her go on and on.

Molly watched Byrd stifle a yawn through the screen door. The porch was deep green in shade.

"Could I put water in the birdbath?"

"Oh, I suppose so."

Byrd's eyes were closed. Probably she was dreaming up new stories to tell Molly after dark, stories of sinners and saints, especially martyrs. Molly was not afraid of the blood in Willie's Bible stories—usually the blood of a lamb, but blood in Byrd's stories could not be easily forgotten.

Molly glanced toward Hi Boy as she walked past the sunporch. She would give him a snack later and maybe teach him a new greeting or even to count. But she lingered, slowly approaching his cage. "There's a place in France," she trailed. She couldn't say it all.

Hi Boy shucked a seed with his hooked bill.

Molly took a shallow breath. "There's a place in France . . . where women wear no pants," she whispered. She repeated it, then walked quickly through the kitchen and outside. He wouldn't remember, she hoped.

Molly followed the stepping stones to the spigot near the garage. She glanced at the back gate leading to the alley beyond, and saw it as a path of escape if lions from the nearby zoo ever bolted from their cages to climb the hills of the neighborhood. From her room at Byrd's, Molly could hear their nightly desire to be uncaged. Their roars kept her aware of her surroundings—a treehouse in a jungle almost. With the exception of the snake that she'd pushed out of her mind, only peacocks had ever escaped. "They like to show off their plumage," Byrd had said once, spreading her fingers in a fan, her diamonds sparkling as she let each finger fall in turn.

Then Molly remembered the dare. Jane had pestered her to throw the new turquoise ring, a present from Byrd, into the grass. Molly had taken off the ring and pitched it just a little way so that Jane would stop urging her. The ring had disappeared into the thatch, and though they had both searched until dark, they never found it. She knew that Jane had been envious. But Molly was, herself, envious. Jane was all that Molly was not.

The stone nearest the water was covered with moss that stained the side of one of her oxfords. She rubbed it with the hemmed edge of her skirt. The spigot lay just inches from the ground making it difficult to fill the can to the top. She would have to make several trips.

The stepping stones that led around to the front of the house were covered in ivy, and daddy longlegs occasionally emerged to walk on leaf tops. The alabaster pedestal supported the bird-bath, looking like a large goblet.

Molly poured the water and thought of Sister Thomasina. Always she lectured the girls about boys. Sister Thomasina would have said that Jane's song suggested an impure thought and that thinking something was the same as doing it. Molly quickly retraced her path humming the "Minuet in G."

When she had finished filling the birdbath, she looked around for a place to watch the flocks soon to visit. She sat on the wrought-iron settee cloistered under an old oak. She crossed her ankles and looked upward. The yellow-white sun shone luminous from behind the leaves like satin through lace. From the house came the sound of "Rosamunde." She sat for a long time waiting for something to happen in the quiet lifelessness of midday, nodding, sliding into a timeless vapor.

And then Jane's face, the warm brown hair, was spinning in her head. Jane was a ballerina dancing in starry spangles of light that swirled all around her, each pirouette a pink blur that drew her closer and closer to a black house lit faintly yellow from within where a hollow voice called.

"Open your eyes, dear." Only Byrd calling Molly to dinner. She got up and went inside.

Her godmother had prepared a feast for the two of them. Molly didn't really care for roast lamb or brussels sprouts, but ate a second helping of sweet potatoes.

Byrd saw her eyeing the charlotte russe on the buffet. "I made it from a recipe in my favorite French cookbook."

Molly wondered what the cookbook would look like. She devoured the dessert, but began to feel uncomfortably full.

"We just have vanilla ice cream at Willie's," she said.

A polite half-smile visited Byrd's face. "No, your grandmother Willie wouldn't know the joys of rich food, I'm afraid."

Byrd sat solidly in her high-backed chair like a queen on a throne. "Are the good sisters telling you the wonderful stories of the Church?"

"Sometimes. Mostly it's catechism."

"You must become *lion*-hearted." She stuck the fork into her charlotte. "I'll try to remember some of them."

Molly knew that the stories crowded her head waiting to be told. Her father had said that Byrd spoke for his side of the family since they were all dead and couldn't speak for themselves. Molly put down her spoon. "What is *lion*-hearted?" She knew the answer but thought that Byrd would like to say it.

"It's being fierce for the faith, dear—like a soldier. It means that you would die for the Lord."

"Grandmother Willie would do anything for the Lord, too," said Molly. "But you're not much alike."

"No," said Byrd guiding a bit of russe toward her mouth. Her lips closed over the cream and moved not at all. Byrd's soldiers would wear red velvet; Willie's, navy gabardine.

Molly thought of Byrd's late husband. "John wasn't a Catholic," she said.

"No, dear. He didn't like 'pomp' as he called it. He said that he saw his God in the eyes of nature. He was a lovely man, but somewhat strange."

"Birds can't talk . . . birds can't talk." They looked at each other. Byrd said, "Always he has to show off." She fussed over the china. "Why don't you pick out a book to read while I put a few things away."

As she walked quickly by the sunporch and into the living room, Molly heard the perch squeak. She perused the tall case of leather-bound books, the collection of John Maclaurin. "What about *Madame Bovary*, Byrd?"

"Wait a few more years for the novels of France, dear." Probably it was on the condemned list, she thought as her fingers glided along the rows, the books smooth and warm to her touch. She stopped on *Rob Roy of Scotland*. John Maclaurin's name was written inside. Scotland was okay. She sat in the big chair and sank into its safety. But as she began to read, she felt the golden eyes of Hi Boy watching her through the bars of his brass cage, the same eyes that once stared at prowling shadows in a dark jungle and sea waves white and treacherous below the night sky. She sat up very straight, remembering when she'd ridden the pony around the ring at the zoo, growing warm with the eyes of the carny boy hot on her face. She did not look up, until Byrd came into the room.

Molly set her book aside. They went on the porch and sat in the wicker rockers. The crickets were very loud and they rocked back and forth to the rising and falling rhythm of their chirps. The moon shone in the water of the birdbath. No birds disturbed the smooth reflection.

"There was a young girl, Agnes was her name, and a lovely looking girl she was too." Byrd had slipped into her story voice, the sound gliding through the darkness. She was an old bird of paradise, her voice a low rich song. "Well, this Agnes was listening to the good words of the good sisters, but the words were swirling about her head, never entering into those places inside of her where they might have smothered the mischief that was growing there." Byrd's eyes were deep blue, wide open and sparkling with light.

"Her mother and father, being of good mind and faith, had provided her with a prayerful house and the best of the things that the Lord provides his lambs."

Molly nodded.

"But you see, the dearest white lamb at any moment might well turn black as coal. And this happened to Agnes when she followed after a black sheep, a sheep so dark that he could move in the night without so much as rippling the eye."

"But how could . . ."

Byrd resumed tiredly. "The Devil. And the worst of it was that after she had fallen under the spell, she did not confess."

Molly wondered how Byrd knew about Agnes not confessing. It was against the laws of the Church that a Catholic should talk of his own sin, except to a priest.

"And on that day, when she was dressed like a saint, Agnes went to mass. For all anyone knew, she held the same sweet innocence that they had seen and admired every Sunday. Made in the image and likeness of the Blessed Virgin." Byrd bowed her head and stopped rocking. She held her hand over her heart. "On this day, as Agnes made for the altar rail as sweetly as ever, she approached Father Matthew with her hands reverently folded and received the Body and Blood of Christ on her red tongue, but when . . . she turned . . . the bile of all hell poured from her mouth in a sight so vile that not one soul could speak . . . struck dumb they were with sin conjured up before them, grotesque and horrible beyond any words."

The shrill cry of a peacock in the zoo startled Byrd. She stared into the darkness for a moment, then smiled at Molly. "I guess I've become too caught up in my own story."

Molly's head felt heavy. Her hands held her knees. "Did Agnes die, Byrd?" She asked, watching her godmother's eyes.

"Oh yes, dear. Dead to heaven and earth."

The snap of a great fan came from the dark. Molly shuddered as though she were cold. She turned toward the birdbath thinking it now too late for bathers.

"You've quite a visitor, dear," said Byrd.

Molly felt an urge to speak of Grandmother Willie. The desire remained as she watched the peacock perched on the edge of the birdbath. He fanned his tail, then dipped his beak in the fresh water.

"His feathers are like Joseph's coat," said Molly.

"The Holy Ghost," whispered Byrd. And Molly felt that it was. She tilted her head. "I don't think he's going to be able to bathe." Nothing seemed quite enough. "I wonder what he would say if he could talk."

"It's better that creatures can't. Outlandish little phrases . . . that's Hi Boy."

"What phrases?" Molly wondered what Hi Boy had said— what Byrd knew.

"Let's just say at one time he must have been exposed to bad company."

"Bad company," Molly repeated. She held herself quite still. The peacock made purring noises, although he had now vanished in the dark. They seemed to be waiting for Hi Boy to utter something—the false time or something worse.

Chapter ELEVEN

Weeks later, on a Saturday in late fall, she lay with her head buried in the soft down of the pillow, but in her dream stood on the edge of a meadow watching the amber grass shift in the wind. She'd dreamed herself *into* and *out of* Willie's. Blowing through the dream was her relief at not having to go there in person. Freely she was catching scarlet leaves floating down from the trees. "Cooing again . . . infernal cooing." The voice flitted into her sleep like a bird. "It's plain as sin. The coughing did it. If it weren't for those filthy pigeons, I wouldn't have lost the baby."

Awakening in the gray light, Molly thought as how her mother wasn't satisfied with just the two children. It was true that Nat had pleased her. Who wouldn't have been pleased with Nat? But then there was Molly, cockeyed as all get out and unable to master the "Tarantella," though the Holy Ghost knew she was trying.

AS ON every Saturday, when the clock stopped she left the house, walked down Theola Avenue to Watkins and caught the Crosstown bus for Willie's. But unlike other times, she was the only white person on the bus. The Negroes sat in the back, taking the seats toward the front only when the bus stopped and let on more passengers. There was some rule about this. From the rows of black faces their talk was a rhythmical rise of melody. Molly imagined herself in Africa traveling with them to the Hardy house, a hut made of wattles stuck in the middle of the jungle. Willie wore a white pith helmet, heavy brown boots and a dress the color of sand as she boarded the bus. She was a missionary. Molly served as her native bearer, toting a heavy pack of Bibles on her back. They were bound for the foot of Mount Kilimanjaro where the revival was scheduled. Willie was disgusted because the tribes of Zulus and Watusis ignored her directive to practice "How Great Thou Art." They were chanting instead the "Kyrie." But she was most pleased when Molly stood up and played "The Old Rugged Cross" on the accordion without a glitch.

MOLLY GOT back home early that afternoon as her family was preparing for the picnic. In the kitchen her mother was poking her chin toward the window, her eyes circling the backyard for a sighting. "I don't see a one, but sure as I'm standing here they're out there milling around, spreading disease." Dr. Blasingame had disputed her claim that pigeons were the reason for her congested lungs. He said she had allergies just like half the people in Memphis. But she clung to the notion that pigeons were at fault and was bent on getting rid of them. She poured the cold coffee down the sink without looking. The stream of brown splashed the white porcelain. She seemed peeved about the wasted coffee as though she wanted to blame that on the pigeons, also. Molly's father had offered to reheat it, but "No," she said, "it's never any good after it separates." The cooing was faint and seemed far away.

He was oiling the hinges on the old wicker picnic basket, wiping the excess with a terry cloth rag. He and Molly both knew that the pigeons were lined up on the largest branch of Mr. Remmler's red oak, hidden behind its bronze leaves, but they said nothing. The hinges squeaked as he worked the lid.

Lena was wrapping the golden brown chicken in waxed paper, securing each piece with a rubber band. "Whoever feeds them old pigeons *won't* after you gets the facts told, Miz Flanagan."

"Off with their heads!" said Molly's father, his own head just inches below the blades of the fan murmuring from the ceiling. He looked over at Molly with slightly raised eyebrows and she took that to mean he hoped someone would always feed the pigeons. Her face felt cool in the air that was stirring.

He closed the lid of his basket. "A lot of stories in there," he said, reweaving some of the stray wicker as if his memories might escape through the holes only to become fragments lost in time. "When I was a boy, we'd ride the train to Raleigh Springs. We held elegant picnics under giant ash trees. Ate paté."

Lena was stuffing eggs and looked up. "Some folks eat chitterlings, Mr. Jim. Ain't much difference in the two, if you're asking me."

"Did I now?" But he wasn't the least provoked that she'd spoiled his memory. Lena's association with the Flanagan family went way back; her father, Distance Mills, was a bright copper penny in his memory bank.

Molly's mother never said what they ate on picnics down at Bullfrog Corner, or if they even had them.

Some of Molly's own memories were held in the basket—her father wearing the army hat that nearly covered his sandy red hair, pitching the baseball, while a June bug tied to the handle buzzed recklessly in circles . . . her mother batting a ball and laughing, and Nat flying a kite gloriously high, reaching for the sun, and herself jumping and pointing at it, stirring up dust on the baseball field baked brown as a sheet cake. All of this lay covered in the worn blue cloth under the lid that kept the sweetness of early days hovering in time.

"I suppose Ludie Finch'll have to come to the picnic. Why Frances Mahon insists on keeping company with her I'll never know."

"Ol' Ludie's not spoiling the day for you, is she, El?"

"I hadn't given it that much thought."

"Amazing how she mixes up her fricatives." He saw that Molly didn't understand and explained that Ludie Finch lisped "z" for "s" and vice versa. "Znores like a znake is my guezz."

Her mother shook her head. She walked into the dining room, the floor yawning and stretching. She didn't get on with his family particularly well, including the Mahons. But she did think they were special and should not associate with ordinary people like Ludie Finch who couldn't even talk like a normal person.

Her father said, "I think Mrs. Flynn and Miss Doyle might join us. Of course they'll bring the rice pudding." He was letting cats out of the bag one at a time, working his way down to Mr. Remmler. "And possibly Tim and Tom."

"Mr. Remmler, too, I suppose," she said, guessing flatly.

"All the more people to hear your speech, my dear. Come on out when you're ready."

Her mother was unhappy about having the picnic in the front yard, but the bayou out back was giving off an unpleasant odor. Her father pointed out that by holding it in the front yard, neighbors who chose not to come might still succumb to her influence, since no doubt they would eavesdrop from their porches when she spoke out against the pigeons.

Molly followed her father outside. Across the street Frances Mahon was having to sweep the front steps in big half circles in order to avoid bumping the broom into her own stomach. "Be over in a minute," she called. Her baby was due soon after Christmas. Molly wondered if she'd be as happy with the second baby as she was with the first.

Next door on the Flynns' front porch the dotted swiss curtains were stretched tautly on wooden frames for drying. Through the thin gauzy material the potted African violets were framed like a still life drained of color. Beyond the Flynns', Mr. Remmler was smoothing the flower bed with the bamboo yard broom as if tending the grave of a dear friend. "Speak to Old Man Remmler," her father said, motioning her toward his yard. Mr. Remmler's wheelbarrow appeared as a bier on which his heap of dead hibiscus rested. Her father went out of his way to speak to people, especially the old ones, but she did not think he would visit Mr. Remmler if the old man were sick in bed.

The day was crisp but warm, the kind that sets doubt in your mind, when a hard laugh barely hides a strange deep pool of tears. Molly remembered Willie's seeds that she'd hidden under her bed. She didn't want her mother to feel responsible for planting them. Maybe in spring she'd give them to Mr. Remmler.

Her father's voice was a vibrant knell that lifted her from a dead calm. "What say, Mr. Remmler?"

The old man tipped his brown tweed newsboy's cap riddled with mothholes. His old blue eyes sparked in the sun. Sprigs of thick white hair stuck out from under the cap when he set it back on his head. "Jim, your iris flags were outstanding this year. Really just the finest." This was the beginning of an old conversation. Her father wasn't much interested in gardening, but gave the old man his full attention.

"I don't know how you got each color into its own row like that."

Last spring the iris flags in the Flanagans' backyard had bloomed in rows of color like the stripes of a rainbow—green, yellow, pink and orange—though the tubers from Willie's heap had given no hint of color before Molly randomly selected and planted them.

"No credit here, Mr. Remmler," he said. "It was Molly's miracle."

"Is that so?"

"There's a bit of story on the iris, you know. The goddess Iris carried messages from heaven to earth using the rainbow as a bridge, which means that the flower iris—her *sacred* flower—and the iris of your eye are symbols of message and communication."

Mr. Remmler's own eyes showed the perplexity of a scientist brooding over one of life's mysteries. He nodded as if he'd known about the goddess all along, but didn't believe any of it. He rubbed at his chin, leaving some of the yard dirt on his stubble. Mr. Remmler accepted fate—that's what he always said anyhow, but the iris presented him with a mystery and he wanted to know the secret. Molly wanted to know it, too, but it was in the air the same as the Holy Ghost. You couldn't see it or grab it, you could only feel it touch you.

Like snowflakes, white droppings were splattered on the bark of the red oak's trunk. Millet the pigeons hadn't yet found dotted the scrub grass. The birds cooed loudly, but were now nowhere in sight.

"Elizabeth heard the pigeons this morning, Mr. Remmler," said her father. "But she hasn't seen you throwing the feed."

"I've taken to pitching it in the garage for the most part, Jim."

"Bright idea, Mr. Remmler," he said, congratulating the old man.

"They're nice pals, Jim. They talk, but you don't have to listen if you don't want to. Maudy and me was mostly like that." Molly wondered why they'd never had children. Once she had wondered aloud if Mrs. Maudy Remmler was buried in the hibiscus bed, so tender and careful a gardener was Mr. Remmler when he worked it. Her father said it wasn't so, that Maudy Remmler was in Calvary Cemetery just like his own dead family.

A lot of statues stood guarding the dead out at Calvary, an assortment of angels and saints—seraphim and cherubim, Chrysogonus and Cyprian; and some apostles, John, Peter, and

Paul—although nobody would ever know whether or not any of their likenesses were even close. If Mr. Remmler'd had money enough he would have erected a statue in honor of Maudy. She felt sure of it. Mama Jo, Clare, and Nate were all buried out there. Her father had said that Mama Jo was a woman of charitable enterprise and that five indigents, not related, were also buried in the family plot, put there by Mama Jo because they had no other place to go, much to the consternation of Grandfather Nate, whom she squeezed to pay the tab for their caskets. The whole bunch was put to rest in the shadow of a huge statue of St. Michael the Archangel standing nearby on top of an Italian. Statues of equal splendor guarded the graves of a horde of Germans and some Poles. Only simple plaques and stones marked the resting spots of the Flanagans. "They'd gone and spent all their money having fun. In the end, angel, there wasn't enough left for the commission of marble saints." Her father had said this, and then a peculiar smile had spread across his face. "And with the intrusion of the five indigents, there wasn't much room left for family members in the plot, so some of them—your grandfather, for instance—were put to rest just outside the little iron fence. He doesn't have a tombstone either, but that's another story." He'd seemed displeased with himself and she wondered why he didn't go on and buy his father a stone.

Mr. Remmler made sure they noticed the "Lost Goose" sign taped on the streetlight in front of his house. The letters of the sign graduated from small to large in the shape of a megaphone. Pete had been missing for three days, and Mr. Remmler suspected that someone had stolen the old bird to fatten him up for Thanksgiving.

"Gonna be a tough chew. That's my thinking," he said.

Molly thought of Lena's vision and wondered if Pete was in *her* pot.

The neighbors were converging in the Flanagans' front yard. Mr. Remmler followed as Molly and her father walked home. Tim and Tom Flynn were setting up three big picnic tables procured from the fire department as Nat unfolded the chairs. Frances Mahon was flapping wrinkles out of the red checkered cloths. Ludie Finch and Jane walked from across the street, each carrying a dish of baked beans. Sue and Jimmy trailed behind them. Mr. and Mrs. Colbert and Charlotte brought two large pans of ravioli and a chocolate cake. Charlotte was wearing her tap shoes and a costume hoping she'd be asked to perform. George Mahon and Alfred rolled the Southern Comfort from across the street in Alfred's red wagon. Lena had helped her father make it, protesting with each peach she'd peeled. Then George Mahon had stored it in his basement. Her father and George served glasses of it and soon the yard was humming.

Elizabeth Flanagan came out and began her speech without warning. She quickly reviewed the roosting habits of pigeons and got right to the heart of her subject, which was the fungus spread by the birds' offal. She quoted a prominent attorney, who in a recent newspaper article claimed to have contracted histoplasmosis from the courthouse pigeons in downtown Memphis. "According to him," she said, "'their droppings are indiscriminate and steady, plainly a menace.'" In the article, he declared war on pigeons and now she was the leader of one of his squadrons.

She stood tall on the front steps and spit five-syllable words out like bullets—"Moratorium" and "Columbiformes." She gained speed as she let out the fluttering of Latin terms that seemed to please Molly's father. But Molly saw that the rest of the group was straining. It didn't occur to her mother to simplify her language.

Ludie Finch was listening hard while smoking as professionally as an actress, her gray eyes dull in the cigarette fog that never did choke her though it nearly strangled everyone else. "They never seemed bad as all that. Just goes to show what all you don't know."

"Although histoplasmosis is respiratory in origin, it can spread to the pulmonary lymphatics and, by the blood, to the mediastinal lymph nodes, spleen, liver, adrenals, gastrointestinal tract, kidneys, skin, central nervous system, heart, and other organs."

"What about the stuff we give *them*, Jim?" asked Mr. Remmler, hiding his mouth with his hand as he whispered. He was jiggering his foot up and down.

"It's best not to mention that now, Mr. Remmler. Lay low, in other words."

"It may be asymptomatic, acute and benign, *or* progressive and eventually fatal," she warned.

Molly decided that her mother had a keen sense of rhythm, but still wondered about all the big words served up at a picnic. Her father poured more of the Southern Comfort for George, the

Flynns, Mr. Colbert, and Mr. Remmler. Mrs. Flynn decided to try it. They all seemed to be listening, but Molly could tell that they wouldn't want to listen much longer.

Elizabeth Flanagan breathed deeply and coughed. "The inhalation of fungal spores—dried, fragmented fungal—from animal proteins such as the aforementioned pigeon droppings . . ."

"What about crows, Elizabeth?" interrupted George, gently shaking his glass. "We have a lot of them around here. Damn things caw all day long." Frances Mahon held her finger in front of her mouth to shush him.

"The evidence will convince you that histo is reality and not just a threat. Especially important for *Frances*, George. Even if *you* don't care." She had a satisfied look on her face like she'd slugged him. "Please all of you line up single file along the walk." She was impatient for all of them to see the fungus in the X-ray and waved her arms to speed them up.

The red checks of the table cloth appeared in and among the ladder of ribs. Frances Mahon agreed to hold up the X-ray. Elizabeth Flanagan picked up a hickory stick. She pointed it between the third and fourth rib, to the area of infection in the lung. The fungus looked like an egg.

"Whose lungs, Elizabeth?" asked Alfred, just needing to talk.

Bristling, she refused an answer, her brown eyes narrowing with an intensity that rippled her eyebrows. As she stared down at him she looked much like Grandmother Willie. It was unlike Alfred to cringe.

"Never mind, Alfred," said Molly quietly. She was wanting to protect him. "She's just sad about the baby."

"I know," he said. "Sad because it's not coming for a million years. Like Christmas." He was looking at Frances.

"Not *your* baby," she said. "Ours. The one Mother lost." Then she realized what she'd said and was put out with herself. And she wasn't about to explain what she herself didn't completely understand. "Just shut up forever."

He rolled his shoulders and backed away, nodding so solemnly that she was sure he'd never speak again.

Ludie Finch was filling up with apprehension. "I hope nothing happens to the children . . . and already I have lung congestion. Probably couldn't stand more."

"If their food disappears," her mother declared to Ludie Finch, "the pigeons will also." She folded her arms and held them firmly. "It's up to all of us to keep our neighborhood safe . . . catch who's putting out the feed." Her chin moved forward three inches, her profile finely crafted in spite of it. "United together, we will ensure that Theola does not become a breeding ground for disease!"

Elizabeth Flanagan's fire and brimstone ending got the Widow Flynn clapping. Under the influence of Southern Comfort she completely forgot herself and spoke to Mr. Remmler. She addressed him by his first name. "Now who in the world would be fool enough to feed pigeons, Hank?"

His face full of wonder, Mr. Remmler raised the bill of his cap and looked toward the sky for the answer.

Like a dam breaking, everyone talked at once. Frances Mahon said, "Paint a sign and nail it to a tree—'Pigeons Prohibited.'"

"Shoot 'um," said Charlotte.

"Guns are illegal in the city, Charlotte," said Mrs. Colbert.

"That's a bit harsh, anyway," said Tom Flynn, who was wearing his uniform and packing a thirty-eight.

"Use a silencer," said Alfred.

"Buy a tomcat from the animal shelter," said Tim Flynn. "Sort of a sentry."

Her father rolled his eyes. "Whatever it takes." He and George were childhood friends as well as cousins. They were rekindling events from times past, the Southern Comfort oiling their memories, and were not concerned about pigeons.

"Form a patrol," said Mr. Colbert. Mrs. Colbert agreed. "It's the American thing to do."

"I'll knock 'um off with my slingshot," said Jimmy, giving Sue a thump on the arm. She tuned up to the high piercing sound of a small dog.

"The boy's mean, Jim," said George. "Takes after his brother Ray." He remembered Ludie Finch and looked over to see if she'd heard him talk bad about her son, but she was engrossed in the X-ray.

"Jimmy's not like Ray," said Jane. Her face was red. "He never would be like that. Jimmy, tell Sue you're sorry." And Jimmy said that he was, but Sue was still wailing.

George picked Sue up and sat her on his knee. Glad for the attention, she immediately stopped crying and said, "We can catch pigeons and take them to somebody else's neighborhood."

"Pass the pigeon," said George. "Share the wealth."

Molly's mother shifted her hips, a sign of impatience. The chatter was beginning to wear on her. Molly's father offered her a glass of Southern Comfort, which she refused. He started teasing her about passenger pigeons.

"That's history, Jim," she said.

"Thursday's novena," said Ludie Finch, short of breath, but sincere in the offering.

Smiling, Frances Mahon said, "Why Ludie Finch, you promised Thursday's prayers for me."

"That's enough pigeon talk," said her father, ready to wrap things up. "Let's have some entertainment. Molly'll play us a tune."

Molly hadn't planned on any such thing and looked at him, wrinkling her face.

"Are you sure she's ready for this?" her mother asked.

"It'll help her get ready for the recital."

Recognizing opportunity, Mrs. Finch said, "Jane, hon, run home and put on your costume."

"Charlotte's all ready for us," said Mrs. Colbert. She was floating in pride.

Charlotte, in blue satin, was sitting there with an innocent face, like she hadn't expected to be asked at all. In truth Molly knew she'd been counting the minutes. Still, Molly felt bad for her. It was unfair when you looked so much like that small dot of stupidity that was in you, as if that dot were the whole of it and nothing more. Dancing side-by-side with Jane, Charlotte was sure to look dumb as all get out.

"Go with me, Molly," said Jane.

Molly looked at her father for permission. "Go along, Molly," he said. "But hurry on back."

Her mother let this pass, but she was frowning.

Mrs. Finch called after them. "Ask Ray to come."

Molly was listening for the possible interchange of fricatives that never came and almost forgot to say "Yes ma'am." She didn't see much reason to ask Ray. Ray never came over to the Flanagans' or any of the other houses in the neighborhood, most likely because he wasn't made welcome anymore than the rest of his family, although Frances Mahon *had* always been kind to Ludie Finch. It was only Jane who managed to slip by the sort of stigma of being common that was attached to the rest of the family. Once in a while Jane sat on the Flanagans' front steps and talked with Molly—okay because her father said so over the objection of her mother—but Molly was not allowed inside the Finch house. Her mother didn't like the looks of Ray, said he wasn't much good. Her father said that Ray Finch was *very* good—at nail paring.

The Finch house looked as deserted as last summer's bird nest. On the front walk Jane stepped on every crack. The porch steps bowed slightly in the middle. Both of them walked up one side. Through the screen door the grayed walls were bare except for the crucifix hanging in the living room above an overstuffed chair. The chair was covered in brown frieze that had split, and yellowed cottony stuffing was taped at the seams. Molly wondered how Mrs. Finch could afford dancing lessons for Jane.

The screen was hooked. Jane hesitated, then knocked. A stack of old newspapers sat by the fireplace along with some sticks for kindling and a big iron poker. The lamp beside the chair had shorted out and was blinking like a warning beacon for barges on the river. Molly watched a cavalcade of ants march up the porch wall. Then the floor was squeaking. Ray Finch was in his sock feet and walking toward them in a lazy roll, not really caring if he got to the door or not. He was fiddling with a book of matches. He looked up and unhooked the screen, then stared at Jane. She opened the door and brushed past him. "Wait for me, Molly."

He quickly hooked the door again and stared at Molly. For a split second he was two-headed. She looked away from him, focusing on her own thumbnail, then back again. He struck a match on the seat of his jeans, held it up for a second, then lit a Lucky Strike. He blew smoke through the screen. "Whatja come over here for?"

It wasn't really a question and she wasn't sure if she was supposed to answer or not. She felt herself the intruder, the Fuller Brush man when you already owned three brushes or the lady selling cosmetics when you didn't even wear lipstick or the Jehovah's Witness when you already had a religion.

She was uncomfortable in the silence. Not knowing what to do with herself, she rocked back and forth. "Just waiting for Jane." The cigarette dangled from his lips. She waited for him to take a drag. "Your mother wants you, too," she remembered to say. "And Nat's over there." She thought it might do Ray some good, being with someone his own age and all, although now that she thought about it Nat never did have anything to do with Ray, except for throwing his paper route once in a while when Ray had gone off with his father.

"Like I care to hang around with a cheat." He struck a match with his fingernail just for something to do, then snuffed it out in the hole of his fist. "The great Nat Flanagan stole my money. He's a damn thief."

Behind the glaze, his eyes threatened and she felt the storm inside of him. She didn't know why Ray was mad, but she would take up for Nat no matter what. "Nat's about perfect," she stuttered. And she almost believed this was so, except for when she thought of Nat and Jane together, ever since that day she'd seen them at the Rosemary. She'd kept thinking of Byrd's story, imagining Jane as Agnes and Nat as the black sheep leading her astray. But even if the worst had happened, Nat wouldn't steal if he was starving. Molly remembered her turquoise ring lost in the grass. "Likely it's Jane, I bet." She heard her voice change like her own mother. When she was truly nervous she slipped up and talked Mississippi.

Ray said nothing, so Molly figured he was beginning to see that Jane had taken his money, that he just hadn't considered it before.

"He threw my route for a week. That's when he got it."

"But you asked him to throw your papers—when you were away with your father."

"I didn't say nothin' about him collecting no money. He flat stole it. Collected for months back and acts like he dudn't know nothing about it."

Ray was just lazy enough not to collect money for his own work. But none of it made sense. Why would Nat do such a thing? And if Nat did do it, why wouldn't Ray just turn around and fight him or tell her mother or father? The planks under her feet were warped and splintered, and she felt herself on shaky ground. Though Molly didn't really believe any of it, she was glad when Jane appeared wordlessly behind him. She wore her blue satin baseball costume from last spring's dance recital, almost too tight for her now, and carried the little bat she used as a prop.

"She's gonna get it back. Right, Sister Jane?" There was an ugliness about Ray that just sat on his face like he'd bought it.

Jane looked him right in the eye and said, "You'll get what's yours soon enough. If you do like you say you'll do." She turned to Molly. "He's not bothering *you*, is he?"

Molly shook her head, but in truth Ray *was* bothering her. Being near him on this porch had made her mightily nervous. But now that the talk of theft was out in the open, Molly wanted to ask about the ring. Jane might have hidden it somewhere in the house. If she told Ray, maybe he'd see to it that Jane returned it. But Molly had never told on anyone before and couldn't find the words now. Her father had said that tattling was against honor.

Jane said nothing more to her brother and danced down the middle of the steps, clicking the tap shoes, fearless of the bowed-up boards. "Hurry up and I'll teach you some dance steps, Molly," said Jane. "Come on."

"Your mother wants you to come, too." Then she remembered that she'd already said this, but Ray didn't look like he was about to come anyhow and she was glad for it. She followed Jane across the street, and without turning around was nearly sure that Ray was watching Jane.

As they returned to the Flanagans' yard Ludie Finch was telling Mr. Remmler how she worried over Ray and how he and Jane seemed to actually hate each other. Across the street Ray had sat down on the steps and was paring his nails. Mr. Remmler said he didn't know much about young people, but hating each other was what they were renowned for and he thought she was worrying needlessly. Ludie didn't seem entirely satisfied with Mr. Remmler's wisdom. She asked Molly's father what he thought about it. "Ray's always standing away from things, always alone, and won't mix for nothing."

Molly thought that Mrs. Finch had asked the wrong person. Except for arguing with her mother over the eye operation, he only discussed pleasant things. "I'm sure he'll come around soon enough, Ludie," he said. Then he turned to Molly and asked what she'd like to play. "Make sure it's something you know," he said.

"The 'Spinning Song,' I guess." It wasn't much of a piece, but she still found the "Tarantella" troublesome.

"Open your windows all the way so we can hear you," said Frances Mahon.

Mrs. Flynn said, "Halfway ought to be plenty."

Nat was whispering to Jane. Molly was surprised he'd talk to her in front of their mother, who would surely question him about it later. Molly wanted to ask him about the money, but instead she went on inside.

The living room was full of sun, a time of day when the ghosts rested. She hoped she wouldn't disturb them with the "Spinning Song." If she and her mother and father and Nat ever moved from this house, she wondered if the ghosts would follow. They were companionable and plain easy to get along with, especially Nate Flanagan whose affable face cheered her from the dark carved wood of the picture frame. No one had ever said how he'd died. Her father always brushed her question aside. Now and again she wondered.

In the hall cabbage roses were blooming out of season on the wall. The air was cooler over the newly installed floor furnace. At times she worried about snakes down there. Already the nights were chilly and soon her father would have to light the pilot. After that her mother would let the bread rise on top of the grate, but just now its crisscross pattern looked to her like a trap.

Lena was dusting away Daniel and the Lion's Den from the face of the piano. Always in the Bible someone was being eaten, burned, or sacrificed. There was no end to disaster. "You play real pretty now, you hear me?" Lena raised the three front windows all the way. "Try lookin' at the notes with both of them eyes."

Molly opened the piano bench and took out the music. After flipping to the right page, with the sketch of an old woman spinning yarn, she thought for a minute and then got up and lowered each of the windows to a three-inch opening, hoping her mistakes wouldn't slip out.

Lena was frowning as Molly sat down and tried to compose herself. "What you go and do that for?"

Nat came in and stood in back of her. "Go ahead," he said. "Don't play too loud . . . you know, just in case."

"Nat, you'll have this girl gone out of here before her time."

Already Molly was uneasy, but Nat's lack of faith in her ability to get through the thing without flubbers was wholly disconcerting. And then Lena was telling her "Never you mind, child" in a gentle voice that suggested she really did need coddling. Suddenly Molly chose irritation over hurt feelings and started playing the "Spinning Song" in the way she liked best—fast and wild. This way she could play over her mistakes before anyone heard—just roll over them—and no one the wiser. She played real loud.

"Keep it down, will you?" Nat was having to holler, but still she could hear his voice. She played louder still, the notes rising out of the piano like a swarm of stinging bees. Midway she was out of control and banging the keys. In the corner of her left eye she saw Lena covering her ears. She should stop—she knew that—but didn't because she was hell bent for the end.

"Lord, Molly. Hell fire." Nat sat down on the bench. "I don't know about you, Molly."

She turned and looked out the window. Her father pretended that her performance was acceptable and clapped moderately, but her mother held both hands over her face. Molly'd disgraced her in front of the neighbors, though most all of them were clapping, if only half-heartedly. "The baby would have been a concert pianist," she blurted. "Just come out knowing how it's done."

Lena and Nat looked at each other. An explanation was forthcoming. Molly could see it forming in Lena's head. "For sure your mama wanted you to know. But you see it was gone before you could count on it coming anyhow. Just the way of things is what."

"You knew, didn't you, Nat?" Molly looked at him. In spite of the deep frown, his face was full of pity.

"I'm three years older than you," he said. "It's over and done."

"Your mama's glad for what she's already got. She just don't hardly know it yet."

Nat sighed and sat down beside her at the piano. He quickly figured out the melody of "Take Me Out to the Ballgame" and played it over a few times. "Molly, go on over and stand by the window. Tell me when Jane raises her bat, but don't let anyone see you."

She did as he said without knowing why. She'd just spent herself playing and didn't have energy enough left for protesting. Out there Jane and Charlotte were standing at opposite sides of the yard on the sidewalk, poised with their bats. Nate played a chord and held it. "The windows," he said. "Open them, will you?"

Lena and Molly did as he'd asked. Then he played a few bars and waited.

"Okay," said Molly. "She's raising the bat."

He played "Take Me Out to the Ball Game" as Charlotte and Jane tapped toward each other. When they got to the center, they went through the routine without a mistake. "And it's one, two, three strikes you're out. . . ." The girls swung their bats and then started the dance. Jane was grand; she danced smoothly and with perfect rhythm. When she reached to the sky, it was as if she were reaching for a star. Charlotte shuffled a couple of times when she was supposed to hop, otherwise she wasn't all that bad. With the ending, Charlotte and Jane "shuffled off to

Buffalo"—really just the hedgerow—and then shuffled back in front of the audience to take deep bows. Everyone clapped. "Jane's very good," Molly said aloud to no one.

Without turning around Nat said, "Someday she might be. If she gets the chance."

The applause was loud and long. "Don't tell who was playing the piano," said Nat, pushing up from the bench. "Keep your mouth shut."

Since Nat was a football player and proud of it, Molly guessed he didn't want anyone thinking of him as a sissy who played the piano. But that didn't make sense either—everyone knew he was an actor and wasn't that show business?

"Why not?"

"Just do like I say."

"Let's hear it for the pianist," called her father from the yard. "Miss Molly Flanagan!"

So that was it. A charade. So all of them would think she'd been the one.

"Molly! I didn't know you could play baseball!" That was George calling. Everyone laughed at his joke, but at the same time they were clapping hard—applauding Molly's performance playing a song she didn't even know! Molly wished Lena would just draw her into Jerusalem.

Nat looked at her and in a quiet voice said, "You owe me one, that's all. You'll get it right soon enough. If you work at it."

Lena hadn't said anything in a while. "It'll just take some time, I'm thinking." But judging from the look that passed between Lena and Nat, sometime might never come.

Chapter TWELVE

"You gotta see this, Molly," said Nat. "The old fossils are dancing."

Her father had put on a stack of records and the "Anniversary Waltz" was playing. George was dancing with Frances, though he had trouble getting close to her. She was light on her feet in spite of the extra load. Mrs. Flynn danced with Tim, Miss Doyle with Tom. Looking on, the other neighbors were gathering dishes and belongings, preparing to go home. Alfred danced with Mrs. Finch.

"Mr. Jim is some kind of dancer," said Lena. "Miz Flanagan's not so bad herself."

Lena was generous. Molly knew her mother didn't like dancing in the front yard. Maybe that was why she seemed so awkward.

"I wish you young people could have seen your grandfolks dance. Miz Clare and Mr. Nate. Now that was dancing."

Molly felt a wisp of a breeze on her face and thought it must be Nate and Clare whirling in circles around them. She couldn't imagine Grandaddy Bob and Grandmother Willie ever dancing, not even the two-step, though in truth Willie had plenty of rhythm in her hands and head.

Her father's hand clasped her mother's waist as if to lift and glide her over any ruts that might trip her. He was about the same age as his own father in the picture, and they looked very much alike. Besides selling insurance, her father collected rent just as his own father had done. "Lena, how did Grandfather Nate Flanagan die? My father never said."

"Now don't be asking me that. It's not for me to be saying nothin' about. And if I were you I wouldn't be asking Mr. Jim. No, ma'am. I wouldn't be asking such."

"He blew his brains out," said Nat.

"But that means he's . . ."

"Don't say it. And don't talk about it to Dad. Not one word. I overheard them talking about it years ago, but I didn't say anything. Not long ago Mother told me, but only because of the old men asking me if I'm Nate Flanagan's grandson . . . after the football games. She was afraid I'd find out what he did from a stranger. Dad hasn't forgiven her for telling me yet."

"E" stood for end. For eternity. They hadn't put the "e" on Nat's name.

"Hurtful times for Mr. Jim and all of them. Sad times I'm telling. . . . That's enough now. You all hear? I'm going for my pocketbook. I see Mr. Jim's about ready for me. Nat, you ask is it time."

"Sure, Lena."

Outside the neighbors were saying good-by. Alone, Molly sat on the purple corduroy bedspread and stared at the piano. At his funeral did they even bother to play the "Dies Irae"? For a lost cause? The germicidal lamp cast a gray fluorescence over the room. Later, when all the other lights in the house were turned off, her room would exist in a realm all its own. She thought of her father, having to know with certainty every day of his life, that his own father was suffering in hell forever.

Her mother called her to come and help. She passed through the hall, stepping over the metal grate and stood in the doorway, holding her eyes away from the picture. The room glowed red as if it might burst into flame, and suddenly she abandoned herself to the face of Nate Flanagan, staring at his eyes that might have been blue. The clock on the mantle was hard in silence. And then she knew for certain; he'd done it on a Saturday.

OUTSIDE, SHADOWS disappeared into the coolness of evening. The streetlamps glowed milky white. Molly helped her father and Nat carry the folding chairs to the garage. She listened for the pigeons, but heard only *ollie ollie in free* in the distance.

Then it was time to take Lena home and her father asked that Molly ride with him. "It's been a long day for your mother. We'll give her some time to herself." Nat was already in the front seat when they got in the car. He rode with them down Theola Avenue and on to Faxon where he got out to collect for his paper bill. She wondered if he'd really stolen money from Ray. Would he steal more?

"See ya," he said. He ran up a walk and across the porch of a customer and was knocking on the door before they pulled away.

When they turned on Jackson Avenue and passed the Tarantinos' store, Molly told Lena about the marionette and how she wanted to make one. Lena didn't believe her when she said it was for Alfred. "Now I wonder just who it for?" she asked, holding her chin as if deliberating over a difficult question. "No matter," she decided. "We could make one. Moses would be real nice. Make the beard with some cotton." She rambled on about the materials—the muslin, the strings, the yarn. Her enthusiasm was growing and Molly knew she'd have trouble converting Lena from Moses holding the Ten Commandments to the marionette that she herself wanted. A dancer.

They drove past Anchorage Street where Lena lived. "I'm right here, Mr. Jim. Did you forget me?"

"No, Lena. I wanted you to stay in the car with Molly while I collect the rent. You won't mind, will you?"

"Oh no, sir. Not missing nothin' but listening to men get theirselves in trouble on the street and that means time in the workhouse and that's the sad truth." Lena spoke in a whisper as delicate as a fine lace collar. She was tall and slim, her hair knotted neatly in a gray bun. Molly knew as well as anything that Lena was a lady and that her mother's rule about not calling black women ladies didn't apply.

"What you keep that old place for, Mr. Jim? If you don't mind my asking, that is."

"Habit, I guess, Lena. And the money just might pay for straightening out an eye that doesn't always *see* what it's *looking* at."

Doesn't *look at* what it *sees* was more like it, Molly was thinking. He had it backwards.

"Molly here had nightmares last time you took her on down there."

"That was years ago."

"Young folks remembers."

Lena was rubbing her hands together. Molly knew she was anxious to get home. Each night she drew Bible stories on the walls of her small house with a black crayon, the work sometimes keeping her up until dawn. Elizabeth Flanagan never would have approved of Molly visiting the house of a colored person, but always her father allowed her to walk Lena to the door and view the progress of the mural. The last drawing she'd seen pictured Lena and Molly on the starboard side of Noah's ark, swabbing the deck. Below, in the belly of the boat, pairs of elephants, tigers, giraffes, and zebras were eating straw under the satisfied gaze of Noah himself. Just above him two doves swung on a perch. Lena had said, "Just you pray that I make it through the Old Testament. Then we'll both of us see to the rest."

Down Anchorage the few streetlights were far apart, each one like the singular strike of a match in the dark. It was black as pitch down there on Anchorage. Black as Hell. Black people were killed down Anchorage all the time, but the newspaper never said much about it.

They passed Lena's church. Lena was an African Methodist Episcopalian. How she managed to be all of those things at the same time was a puzzle. Lena had no one but Molly, she was thinking. Unless you counted all the dead people in the Bible. As they drove toward the river, Molly was wishing that Lena could live in the Holy Land like she wanted, and away from the pitch blackness of Klondike. Darkness was more than just the absence of light.

THE FLANAGAN lot on Theola was not the only property they'd gotten from Nate Flanagan. And now, as they entered a part of Memphis that was even darker, poorer, than Klondike, Molly remembered that time when she was sitting between her father and Nat in the car and how as they came up to an enormous building—inherited from Grandfather Flanagan—her father had chanted an odd refrain. It had sounded funny, but no one had laughed.

Uh-Rufus, Uh-Rastus, Uh-Johnston, Uh-Brown,
Uh-What ya gonna do when the rent comes roun?

It was as if to bolster himself, but his voice had not found strength.

And now, as they drove through the streets filled with ramshackle buildings, she moved back in time and felt the same loss of hope. He did not chant now and she was glad for it. He stopped the car and got out. The wind began to rise. "I won't be long," he said, looking toward Lena. Then, as if forced to speak, he turned to Molly and said, "Angel, it's somewhat grim. Don't worry over it." He locked the car and walked away into the darkness.

But she did worry over it. The shame of night was all around her. No matter the reason, he owned this building. It was huge and swayed in the wind, the boards sounding a slow and steady groan under the loud talk of ragged colored people hanging out of windows blazing with red light against the night's purple blackness. A boding, gray and inherent, called out from the deepest silence within her. But it wasn't the fear of blindness from the operation paid for with money ill-gotten that gripped her. The quiet in the car swelled and held her breathless.

And Lena said, "Oh my." And that was all.

The door of the building opened to smoky blue light and her father was let inside. Someone was playing a piano, the tune a raging thunder of low-down notes. The dark closed behind him. And she feared as she waited that her father might never come back.

Chapter THIRTEEN

Anxious to put the day aside, her mother had unpacked the picnic basket and was putting it on the top shelf of the small pantry when Molly and her father returned home. "What a relief," her mother said. "I'm glad that's over."

Molly was glad also, but still anxious. They had driven home in silence after her father had taken an interminable time to collect the rent and come back to the car. Now he was washing his hands at the sink, the lathering of soap a rich frosting. He was fastidious about such things. She was wishing he'd wash his hands of the dirty money when the screen door of the kitchen rattled with a knock.

"Mr. Remmler," said her father. "What's up?" He was rinsing off the soap.

"Jim, you'd better come down right away."

He dried his hands with the towel, rolled down his sleeves, then walked outside with the old man. "What's it all about, sir?"

"You'll have to see for yourself, Jim. I don't know how to tell you." Mr. Remmler's hands were shaking. He walked stiffly.

Molly followed them outside, walking a few feet behind. The old man pointed toward his garage, the dim light shining through the cracks. They passed through Mr. Remmler's gate and into the backyard. Leaves crunched under foot. The heavy garage door groaned in the wind and the rusty hinges creaked.

"Don't go further than the door, Jim."

The yellow light fell on their eyes. Her father quickly hooked one hand under Mr. Remmler's arm and braced himself against the splintered door frame with the other. Wrapped around the rafter, its long body beaded with pigeons, the python watched them, its flat gray skin silver, then blackening, as the yellow bulb swayed back and forth in the wind. Molly heard footsteps from behind, a quick breath, then saw her mother's face touch her father's back. Her arms were clasped around his chest, her body shuddering against him. Faint utterances of birds, clustered on the high beam, threaded the darkness.

PART THREE

Chapter FOURTEEN

The warm winter rain fell solemn and steady as a litany. Nat walked with Molly to the bus stop, although he normally ran to his high school, which was in the opposite direction. Why he was doing this she wasn't sure. Her mind was full of Grandfather Nate and empty of guesses. Water bubbled up from the grates, gurgled, and streamed down the street. Nat was not talking.

The whole of fall had been hot, the leaves holding on to their greenness in a way that seemed selfish. Instead of allowing the gradual showing of red, gold, and bronze, they had suddenly turned brown and died in the way that Nate Flanagan had done when her father was a young man. This was on her mind, so much so that the python merely slithered along the edges, though it, too, never fully left her consciousness.

That night, her father and Mr. Remmler had quickly closed the garage door and held it shut with the stack of bricks. When the Flynns arrived, they opened the door only to discover that the huge snake had escaped through a hole in the back wall. The python was nowhere to be found when the zookeepers came to catch it. Speculation was that it had found refuge in the bayou and might live there happily for years to come, feeding on rodents and small animals—depending on the temperature; if the weather turned cold, it might seek warmth under a house.

Weeks had passed and still each time she looked at her father she thought of the suicide. For Molly it lay close by like a ghostly Grim Reaper. Every day after school she practiced the piano. Often she'd wander from the "Tarantella" into a haze of daydreaminess only to wake with the sound of her own fingers picking out the "Dies Irae." She pictured herself at the recital dressed in a flowing black hooded robe. Lighting the keyboard with flickering uncertainty, the tall white candle burned down to a stub before she finished playing the whole of the *Requiem Mass*. The audience moaned. Now as she walked in the rain beside Nat, she was certain the recital would be the death of her.

Nat had told their mother that Molly knew about their grandfather. "There's always the chance he was *sorry* just before he died," her mother had said to her, pretending that Nate Flanagan might *not* be in hell.

Molly stepped off the curb and into water up to the top of her shoes. The rain pelted her black umbrella. She was holding it awkwardly, trying not to stab Nat with the broken spoke. "I think he was sorry and all," she said, feeling the squish of wet socks. "So what do you think?" She'd asked him before. He never would answer.

"Molly, he parked his car in front of the funeral home and shot himself in the head. He meant to do it." She saw the watery glaze in the corner of his eye and hoped that it was the rain.

"I just meant that, in a split second, he could have just blinked sorry," she said. "He *might* be in Purgatory." She wanted to believe this. Wanted to believe it very badly. "Mother thinks it's possible."

"Mother thinks black and white," he said matter-of-factly. "She doesn't even believe in the rosary, much less Purgatory."

Molly didn't know how he'd gotten so smart. After all, they had the same parents. But he was right. Even though their mother was a convert, she held on to certain things Methodist. Maybe it was better to just be born something and not tamper with it.

"We never knew him, ever, so what's the difference he blew his brains out? Look, I'm plain tired of it. I don't want to think about him anymore. And there's plenty of other stuff for you to worry over. Just keep an eye out for the python. It's the here and now."

"I'm not afraid," she said. Her own eyelashes were damp feathers.

"Fine, then. Worry about your recital or something. Just don't keep asking me what not one fucking soul can answer." He was purely sick of her, she knew that, but he looked toward her as if there was something more. He stopped short and ducked under her umbrella. She held it up high to cover them both. His voice was caught up there, under the dome. "There's just one thing. Don't go near Ray Finch. He's worse than any damn python. I mean that."

And then she saw what she'd tried so hard not to look at. "What about Jane? Something's wrong. I know something's wrong."

He was holding his books inside his old tan raincoat with one hand and squeezing water out of his hair with the other. "I promised never to talk about it and I won't."

Guardian of trust. Unyielding as fate. Molly understood about secrets, sacred things that at once tied you to the giver and set you apart from everyone else.

They were crossing over the bayou bridge when he turned back and headed for his own school. She watched him from the bus stop as he began to lope. At first he seemed barely able to lift his long legs, dragging them heavily behind him. He tucked the two school books under his arm like a football, a fullback now who didn't even care that the books were getting soaked. He busted through the low-lying fog that skirted away from his zigzag path as he dodged players that only he could see. Then he disappeared over the crest of the bridge. The rain hit hard on her umbrella, the sound a loneliness that she understood, and if she could have stayed there for a while, she would have seen its face.

She swallowed hard as the bus pulled up, and wished there was time enough left for walking to school. Riding through the fog, she hardly recognized what street she was on. The world seemed to stand still while the rain played its symphony of sadness; and with the rocking of the bus the movements were the songs she'd come to know: the damping off of the baby, a tinkling nursery rhyme; the sin of her grandfather, a song of lament; and the secret of Jane, a warning song. Her father's song was one of deep abiding troubles, his own and those of the people now living in the wreckage that had come to him out of his past. The sky poured, and the street began to flood—and then she imagined herself alongside the Volga boatmen, pulling boats down the shallow Volga River, headed for the Caspian Sea. "Aye-yookh-nyem! Aye-yookh-nyem!" Willie worked the heavy rope beside her and both of them wore Russian peasant dresses banded in red, black, yellow, and green. The two of them pulled the boatload of passengers—some wounded, some dead, some in danger. Her gnarled old hands strong and sure in the toiling, Willie counseled Molly to sing steadfastly and in a voice moderate but audible. "Aye-yookh-nyem!"

LITTLE FLOWER School rose from the corner of Jackson Avenue and Belvedere. The school's dark-stained trim framed the large windows that looked out on the neighborhood of small houses and old shrubs. Little Flower was a nickname for St. Theresa. Giving a saint a nickname seemed irreverent, but that was the accepted name of the school as well as the church next to it. Molly got off the bus and walked across the street. She felt the pangs of hunger from fasting since midnight as she opened the heavy bronze doors, which remained as evidence that the building had once housed both church and school.

The bell was ringing. Quickly she walked to the classroom, dumped her books, and, outside again, darted under the arched walkway that led to the church. Inside, she slipped into the pew and joined her class, fingering her missal. Some day she might have to read the pages in braille. She read the Latin side, understanding little, but the words were full of music that made glossy an otherwise dull mass.

After the Consecration, she went up to the altar rail, received the Eucharist, and then found her place and knelt down, saying as many prayers to Jesus as she could muster. Afterwards she apologized to the Holy Ghost and asked for protection against blindness.

When she looked up, Jane was coming in late, the wet strands of her hair dripping beads of water as she stepped into the Communion line with the rest of the eighth-grade class. The rain plip-plopped on the high roof and rolled down the stained-glass windows, kaleidoscopes of deep blue, red, and purple. Molly listened for thunder. The Communion of the mass had become the crescendo that swelled out of her own growing uneasiness, some of it the consequence of Byrd's stories, and she hoped now—as she'd hoped for weeks on end—that bile and blood would not pour from Jane's mouth.

IN THE classroom dreams poked into the flat light of the somber day, shifting and darting with the opening and closing of books and the sound of voices. Between lessons of history, English, and math, Sister Mary Thomasina spoke incessantly on the virtues of faith, hope, and charity, making it hard to hear the song of the rain.

In the cafeteria, she sat with Mary Haggarty and watched Mrs. Portugal, the dietician, as she chastised Sam, the black janitor, for being "slow." The pedestals on which the saints had once stood when the cafeteria was still a church remained like Roman ruins. What would the place become next, as the years passed and all of the lunches were eaten? A bomb shelter—"duck and cover," they'd sing—or a hospital maybe. Sam pushed the big mop over a sea of spilled grape juice, the long hairs gradually soaking up the purple swill. Even after the floor was spotless, Mrs. Portugal kept harping about his laziness. Molly felt the peanut butter ball in her throat. Mary was eating tuna and didn't seem to be listening, congratulating herself instead for not having to buy Mrs. Portugal's macaroni and cheese thick as yellow-brown glue. Molly stopped eating altogether when Mrs. Portugal accused Sam of "niggardliness" in such a way that made it clear what she really wanted to say and her getting away with it because, as always, Sister Martha, the principal, wasn't around to hear. Sam's eyes filmed over in a protective glaze.

"Mingo Tingo" Angelo sat across from her, fidgeting because the rain kept him from venting his great energy on the play-ground, where on dry days he would pound the dirt in his primitive dance, dust rising with his passion until it resembled a whirlwind, while everyone clapped and shouted. Sister Thomasina said he had Saint Vitus's dance. But Sister had over-looked that Mingo was Italian; it was clear to Molly that his behavior was inspired by the "Tarantella." The notes of her recital piece played in her head as she watched him wriggle.

Back in the classroom, Sister Thomasina cut the recess period short because of the noise and called a special meeting of the Boy Saviour Regiment that she opened with the prayer, "Dear Boy Saviour, Bless My Behaviour."

Then they all turned toward the big banner hung from a pole in the corner of the room—bigger than the American flag next to it—and saluted the larger-than-life face of the Boy Saviour. "My Captain," they said in unison. "My Model."

In spite of the badge pinned to the navy blue bolero of her uniform, Molly wasn't a real member. Whenever they took the oath of allegiance she would only move her lips. Anyhow, commitment to the regiment didn't seem to improve the conduct of the avowed participants. The sergeant at arms, Ed Riker, had been stripped of his Boy Saviour badge for talking, then beaten on the back for denying it. Sister called her pommeling "Catholic Action" and brushed her hands together when she finished with him as if she'd just whipped the Devil. Other wayward class members, the "lazy lumps," the "bumps on a log," and especially the "gumps" received like treatment. Today when she broke her ruler on Mingo's head—he had stood up and shuffled when her back was turned—everyone laughed. Molly merely smiled. She thought it was funny all right, but somehow the laugh felt like lead down in her chest and wouldn't come on out. She'd carried Nate Flanagan all day long and he had grown more heavy with each passing hour.

At the end of school, when she looked forward to giving herself over completely to the rain and its secrets in the solitude of her own room, she remembered the eye exercises downtown and felt very tired. Even playing the scales was better than the dread exercises. Missing the eye exercises was the same sin as missing mass on Sunday, or worse, the music lesson on Saturday.

So instead of walking home in the rain, where her thoughts might skip back and forth in time—swinging through the jungle, sitting around the Round Table, finding the gate of a secret garden, and sailing on the sea—she waited with the crowd of wet, shiny raincoats under a ceiling of black, yellow, and red umbrellas. The bus plowed through the water, splashing her ugly brown oxfords before stopping. Then she became a yellow fish inside the belly of the whale that had swallowed her.

She sat beside Jimmy, and behind Jane and Charlotte. Jimmy raised and lowered the umbrella until Jane looked over her shoulder and frowned at him. Then she began rambling on and on about the dance recital that was coming up soon. Molly knew Charlotte's ears were wide open as two windows in spring. Their costumes, now being made, were of velvet.

"What color?" Molly did not want to think of the eye exercises. Or her own recital and what she'd wear then.

"Red," said Jane. "For Christmas." She looked back at Molly. "So why do you go downtown every week anyway?"

"Her eyes don't match," answered Charlotte abruptly. She was irritated with the question and wanting to get on back to the dance recital. She pointed her index fingers parallel. "They're trying to get both of her eyes looking at the same thing."

Jane nodded as if she'd known the reason all along. Jimmy turned toward Molly and crossed his eyes. Molly sighed. At her own recital she'd just wear the school uniform.

"Stop it, Jimmy," said Jane, "or I won't go home with you." Jimmy uncrossed his eyes and nervously tapped the umbrella on the floor of the bus. "I'll ride on downtown with Molly," she said. "Just *keep* riding and never get *off.*"

"Don't," Jimmy blurted. "I won't let Ray fuck you."

As much as anything, the word "fuck" out of the mouth of a little kid stunned them into silence. Jane sat still as a statue. Charlotte rearranged her books. Molly stared straight out the window, but in the corner of her eye could see Jimmy's hand held over his mouth as if he was scared he might say it again. Jane finally broke silence. "Ray hits, but he hasn't done anything else. It's what he *says*."

"Don't tell him it was me saying anything," said Jimmy.

Charlotte spoke up. "It's stupid not to tell your mother."

"I tried," said Jane. "She wouldn't listen—just started in on the rosary. The sorrowful mysteries."

Only the day before, Molly had seen Ray slap Jane. They were arguing on the front porch just as their parents had often done. Molly had flinched when, from all the way across the street, she'd heard his hand hit Jane's face, the sound hard and flat like a book hitting linoleum. Most likely Ray figured slapping was his job now that Mr. Finch—who did the slapping when he was loaded—was no longer present. And now Molly knew there was much more. She thought of Jane going home and Ray there waiting to slap her again, or worse. She didn't want Jane's song to be "Élégie," but there it was—the melody canting in her head.

The bus stopped in front of the Tarantinos' store. Charlotte, Jane, and Jimmy all got up. No one spoke. Jimmy slid down the rubbery aisle, squeaking his wet shoes and sending shivers down Molly's back. Charlotte opened the yellow umbrella and headed for the Tarantinos' store where she'd spend the rest of the rainy afternoon gorging on candy, watching Punchinello perform and being wholly pampered by her grandparents. Molly was thinking that Charlotte's life was one long happy song, maybe "Sonatina."

As they crossed the street, Jane and Jimmy each tried to open their umbrella, but it was stuck closed. Riddled with holes, it wasn't much good anyhow. Jimmy gave up and ran on toward home. Jane stopped on the crest of the bridge and stood gazing into the water like something startling might be down there, maybe the python. Then she threw the umbrella into the water. She was getting plenty wet and still standing there as the bus pulled away. Molly couldn't help thinking that bad as it all was, at least Nat hadn't been the one.

The bus slowed to a stop. Through the veil of water pouring down the window, the old Gartley-Ramsey Hospital way back from the street looked as a mansion, a restful and serene retreat. Men usually sat out there in the sunshine with crossed legs, swinging their dull brown shoes up and down with the tic-tocking steadiness of a metronome, eyes fixed and gazing at the blue ball that sat on top of a concrete pedestal. Her father had said that they stayed there at the hospital for however long it took to dry out from the whiskey. Maybe that was where Mr. Finch had gone. Wet and gleaming, the blue ball reflected the black branches of the hickory tree hovering above it, and seemed magical. If Mr. Finch looked into the ball would he see the clear reflection of the real world where Jane was needing help, or would he see only a hazy blue dream?

Molly felt herself sinking into the grayness of the day, a chamber of music where a cello played a bleak and somber "Londonderry Air," just the one lone sound. Then down the aisle of the bus came a black woman wearing rhinestone-studded gold shantung pumps that wanted to dance. She had slipped them on just before depositing her token. She stepped lightly toward the back of the bus, her wet shoes tucked under her arm in a brown paper bag, her hips swaying. Everyone was looking at her shoes. "Queen shoes," said a man in the back of the bus.

Molly thought of Lena, how as a girl all she'd ever wanted was a pair of gold shoes like the ones worn by the dancers in the Rabbit Foot Minstrel Show. That's what she'd said. It was hard to imagine her wearing such shoes. But as Molly rode along listening to the jokes, the stories and the humming—all from the back of the bus, all of it *legato*—she imagined Lena beside her, the two of them traveling with a troupe of minstrels. Molly and Lena both wore pink coats, and pants striped in the colors of the rainbow. They blackened each other's faces with cork. They fastened the yellow ties of their golden tap shoes, which shone brightly in the darkened wings of the stage, while the band played a tune in ragtime. Molly was plenty nervous, but Lena said, "God makes your face, but you make your own smile. You the one responsible for that." The two of them then smiled and danced like crazy. The black audience never guessed that Molly was white, the whites never knew that Lena was black. Dressed in pink satin, Willie accompanied them on the piano and wore her own original face that was hard frowning. But she played the piano wildly and the audience was wowed!

The wipers on the front window brushed back and forth, sweeping the curtain of rain aside. At the next stop Ronnie Rosemary boarded the bus, his jacket dripping as he made a long wet search in the pocket for his token while the driver patiently waited, and the rain beat down steadily. Ronnie wore black high-topped tennis shoes like a small boy's. He stumbled down the aisle and sat on the seat in front of her. His scalp was pink beneath the same old red cap that covered only half of his big head. As the bus pulled away, Molly worried over him being loose on the streets of Memphis.

"He surely has it, all right. The affliction, you all understand now. But I tell you I know on sight that boy's harmless as a fly." It was the black woman with the shantung shoes who spoke from behind. "Don't you be staring none," she said to her friends as though they were mere children. "He might act up some if you go on staring." Since Molly was behind him and out of range if he started flapping the wool hat, she felt safe enough.

For a few seconds hail bounced off the sidewalk like ping-pong balls. Ronnie looked out the window and started bobbing up and down on his seat, garbling a cheer for the hail. Then he stopped short, but not because he felt the eyes of the bus driver looking at him in the mirror. His attention just seemed to give out. Molly wondered how safe was he to be around, and if he had feelings. He was now pushing a tune through the space between his front teeth with his tongue and sounding like a kazoo.

Downtown she got off the bus, crossed Main Street and headed toward the Exchange Building for the eye exercises. Her mother called the bad eye "errant" as if it were French and unrelated to the rest of her. For the most part Molly ignored the cockeye, but heading to the exercises she couldn't dodge the problem of ownership. It was hers the same as those parts of her that were really well done, like her ears. Her ears were small and flat, and both of them were identical, like twins.

The rain had stopped for the most part, the clouds thick and billowing. Above the crowd of black and tan raincoats, the tall hat of the Planters Peanut man nodded as he gave small scoops of nuts to the passers-by. Stepping into the flow, she held out her hand as she was swept past Mr. Peanut. The scoop of peanuts felt hot, and somehow comforting. She blew them cool through the little spaces she made between her fingers. Lena's insistence that peanuts could bring death to the house bothered her, but not enough to stop her from eating them.

She passed under the round black clock that didn't keep correct time and then, inside the building, scooted into the crowded elevator. The doors clanged shut. The back side of the operator's gloves were bright white, the palms worn as an old lion's paws. Behind the safety gate—a crisscross of bars moving back and forth as the operator started and stopped on each floor—Molly breathed deeply, trying to buoy herself for the exercises. Then she was sorry for the breath, as the sweet smell of a cigar filled her head and traveled down to her stomach, turning it over and over again, her eyes blurring as raincoats moved into and out of the cage.

Up on the seventeenth floor, the therapist, Mrs. Goforth, waited in her office, stolid behind her desk. She was wearing a green suit. She watched Molly's eyes as she came in the door. As always Molly looked down to see if Mrs. Goforth's shoes matched her dress. As always, it was so. Molly's mother had said that she wasn't surprised Mrs. Goforth owned so many shoes, much as she charged for the exercises. Molly's father had agreed, adding that if they went ahead with Molly's operation—he was pressing her hard now—they would no longer be forced to underwrite Mrs. Goforth's frivolous purchases of footwear.

"Hello, Molly," said Mrs. Goforth. "Pull your eyes together and look straight ahead. At my nose." She never wasted a minute.

Molly was not ready. Her eyes kept glancing back and forth from the petite green shoes to her own oxfords, big and brown. Under the fluoroscope at the shoe store even the skeletal bones of her feet looked big. Seeing your own bones was peculiar.

Mrs. Goforth cleared her throat and tapped one of the green shoes. Molly tried to look at her nose, which was large, thinking at the same time how her own nose was medium size, but that somehow her feet were the biggest in the class. She was also in the running for tallest—not just among the girls, but also the boys. Either Molly or Mary Haggarty was relegated to last in line for the processions, depending on which one had grown tallest just before each Holy Day. For the last several weeks Molly had slumped her shoulders, ducked her chin and practiced bending her knees in an effort to appear shorter; Christmas and the procession at midnight mass was only a month away and she wanted to get a jump on things. But she sensed that Sister Thomasina would not be fooled. Then too, Mary Haggarty, in a feat far greater than her own, had recently begun curving her neck into an "S" like a swan's, which reduced her height by at least five inches.

She found herself looking down at the brown oxfords again when Mrs. Goforth said, "Any time now, Molly. Look straight at my nose."

"Sorry," she said, and looked up.

Mrs. Goforth was holding up that same old yellow number two with the snubbed eraser that Molly despised as much as she did Willie's metronome. She wavered it there in front of her face. Molly wanted to grind it to sawdust in the pencil sharpener. Mrs. Goforth said, "As I move the pencil toward you, keep looking directly at my *nose*. If you are looking straight, you should see two pencils—one on each side of it."

Molly looked hard, but had trouble focusing her eyes, though she finally sighted the one pencil between a pair of Mrs. Goforth's big noses. "*One* pencil," said Molly. "*Two noses*." She failed to swallow either the laugh sputtering her lips or the cackle that leapt from her throat. Mrs. Goforth was steaming.

"We'll come back to it later." Mrs. Goforth's dignity was ruffled. She then held the pencil up higher, like a flagpole and said, "Now, put your finger in front of your nose and look directly at the pencil. If you can see your finger on each side of the *pencil*, it means you are looking straight."

Molly felt foolish saluting a pencil. She pretended to see two fingers just to get on with the whole business. It was bothersome as well as difficult and soon the weariness would bring on confusion and she'd come to the part where she'd not even remember which one of her eyes strayed. In truth she doubted the possibility of any improvement, ridiculous as it all was. Besides, her mother and Mrs. Goforth exaggerated the problem.

"You need to do this several times a day," said Mrs. Goforth. "It will strengthen your *bad* eye." She said "bad" as though the eye were a sin. Molly guessed she was supposed to feel ashamed, that she should confess the eye.

"Time for depth perception."

She had never really understood what it was about, depth perception. That was the worst of it.

Mrs. Goforth led her to the screen that sat on a table. She slid in an aerial photograph of what looked to be downtown Memphis, turned on a light that illuminated the buildings, then handed Molly a small pointer.

"Which building is closest, Molly?"

She really couldn't say and didn't care to know. She was busily looking for the Cossitt Library on Front Street where she was going if she ever got out of here.

"Which one?"

Molly pointed to what seemed a likely prospect, the tallest of the buildings.

"No, Molly. That's the Sterick Building."

So the photograph *was* of Memphis. So where was the Lincoln American Tower and the Porter Building and Kress's? "That's where *we* are," she said pointing to the Exchange Building. She could see the top of the clock, but not the time, which was permanently six-thirty. The photograph didn't show Court Square either, but she knew people were down there feeding the pigeons. She felt encouraged when she spotted the peak of the Cossitt's bell tower, the library a big red sandstone castle ribboned up high with gargoyles, a chorus of storytellers.

"I don't think you're trying, Molly." Behind Mrs. Goforth the row of medical books were lined up on the shelves according to color: reds, blacks, greens, browns.

When she got over there, to the library, she'd walk under the arched doorway—her father called it "Romanesque"—and then across the marble entryway that was at the same time chilly and warm. The corners were deep in shadow, the dark moodiness a snoozing grandfather in a dimly lit study, full of wisdom, cranky and almost inapproachable, yet summoning with a gesture, the slight raising of a hand.

"Some time this year, Miss Flanagan."

Outside the rain dripped lightly. The sky wore a heavy beard. More wrong guesses and finally Mrs. Goforth heaved a sigh, and said it was time to go. Molly jumped up to leave, opening the door, but before she could get out Mrs. Goforth said, "Have your mother call me. This isn't working. . . . I think we may have to take the more stringent approach to save that eye."

SHE WATCHED the Mississippi flow by from a wooden bench in the dusty corner of the library crowded with books and brown with quiet. Outside the train rumbled over the wet tracks in a hard pulsing rhythm. A hobo sitting cross-legged on top of a boxcar waved. And she wondered if he was going someplace or had he already been, and was there a difference? On her lap was a book about marionettes. She felt the need to read it—and the three more books she was allowed to check out—as quickly as possible. She closed her eyes. The operation, she thought. So now it's come to that.

Chapter FIFTEEN

When Miss Doyle and Mrs. Flynn heard about the eye operation they made enough rice pudding for dozens of after-dinner desserts. The Flanagans were still working on the enormous bowl they'd made in honor of Molly's birthday. Her father suggested she peddle some of it to the neighbors (and wondered aloud how much they'd have to consume when Molly got home from the hospital).

Molly walked down to Mr. Remmler's house to offer him a bowl of it, but he wasn't at all interested in second-hand pudding. "Molly, the one thing I don't miss about Maudy is that damn pudding she always made. Throw it in the bayou. I promise not to tell a soul, especially not those two old mistresses." Mr. Remmler said "mistresses" like he meant something bad. She thought he was just tired of being ignored by the two women.

Molly put the bowl down and sat in his swing, rocking back and forth to get it going. He had set the chain up high to accommodate his long legs and nobody else's could reach the porch floor.

The operation was heavy on her mind. She was glad that the piano recital had been put off, but felt time running out as she swung back and forth. The sun cut through the chill.

"All that hair over yonder makes my eyes tired," he said, rubbing his face. "Strong color will do that to you."

Tim and Tom Flynn were nailing down loose boards on the house, the sound like the beating of drums.

"Looks like they might be finished soon," she said, just keeping him company. Charlotte was tap-dancing next door, practicing for her recital. Molly tried to swing in counter rhythm.

"That's an old house," he said. "Takes a long while to settle a house." He paused to light his pipe that he only smoked in winter. "It took Maudy and me nearly fifty years. Then she up and died." His legs were crossed, the free foot jigging up and down nervously. "Just like a woman," he said. "Always some surprise."

Tim Flynn carried an old doghouse from the backyard and heaved it into the van. Mrs. Flynn hadn't ever had a dog that Molly could remember, but she guessed there had been one sometime.

"I remember the last time I moved a thing," he said. "It wasn't just a doghouse though, mind you." He drummed his fingers on his bony knees, making a hollow sound. He was waiting for her to ask about the moving.

Charlotte was still tapping, but to what song? Molly listened to the rhythm, trying to figure it out. Some Christmas song, she guessed. "What was that?" she finally asked.

He looked hard at her, making sure he had her attention. "Well, now." He was still working on the pipe, sucking it. "It was a big one for sure. It was big enough." He cleared his throat, taking his time like in a movie when it's building up to something. Molly was getting somewhat curious, whereas before there had just been the blank space.

"By God, it was a whole house!" he announced loudly, hoping to startle her. And she was sort of surprised. "An entire big house. Bigger than this one."

In truth his house wasn't big, but Molly could see how moving it might present a problem.

"Back then we had to move them by hand." He folded his arms limply, no longer responsible and glad for it. "Of course we had jacks. Each man of us had one."

"Like changing a tire?" she asked, doubtfully.

"That's it. We placed each man a few feet apart from the next and then we jacked the house up at the same time. That is, after we'd counted down from one hundred. Took a while to get up steam, you see. We got down to zero, and then we jacked it up and carried it on to the other side of the street."

Moving a house just across the street seemed a lot of trouble and effort for the outcome, but then some people make unreasonable demands.

The Flynns were raking the few remaining leaves left from fall. Most of them had blown into the neighbors' yards.

"I'd like very much to see them do it," she said about the house. Doing the impossible seemed important.

Lena opened the Flanagans' louvered door, came out on the steps and looked down the street, finding Molly. The apron was gathered around her thin self, a small dark flower circled in big yellow petals. Her fingers played the air with a sense of immediacy. She hadn't gotten the word that Willie had postponed the recital because of Molly's operation. Though Molly was still made to practice, she secretly felt she'd received a stay of execution. The recital was now scheduled for early January, and she knew Willie would make her play then, even if she could no longer see the music. Looking now at Lena, she realized she might never see the completed mural. Somehow she felt the same as being Michaelangelo's apprentice—when the ceiling was almost done, being barred from the Sistine Chapel. She would keep Lena's art in memory, rolling it in her mind over and over again, like an old and often repeated story.

"Good luck with the music," said Mr. Remmler as she slid out of the swing and picked up the bowl. He screwed up his mouth at the pudding. He'd forgotten to cut the hair growing out of his ears and was starting to look disreputable. "If it was me, I'd just bury it in the ground. Feed the worms."

She thought about suggesting the pudding for the few pigeons he had left, but decided against it. He'd suffered enough. She hopped off the steps and ran down to her front yard, holding the pudding to her side so the Flynns wouldn't notice. Like it or not she'd have to eat it.

In the living room Lena was corralling peanut shells that had spilled over from her father's ashtray. Molly glanced at the pictures of Mama Jo and Clare, closing her eyes to Grandfather Nate.

"No peanut shells," Lena said, brushing her superstitions from the table into her hand.

"You might as well leave the shells," said Nat. "He's bound to eat more before the day's over."

"I'll worry over the new shells when I see them," she said with a sigh. "Anyhow Mr. Jim's busy under the house making his adjustments to the pilot light right now."

"Dad has no mechanical ability," said Nat shaking his head and turning the page of his book. He was reading *Moby Dick*.

"Maybe he's not the only one. I don't see you out there helping." Lena put the shells in her apron pocket and went on with her dusting, but held tight to what bothered her. "Like I told you, pecan shells ain't of particular importance. It's the peanut shells what spells trouble."

"I don't get it," said Nat, distracted now from his reading.

The true meanings of Lena's remarks were like the keys she wore tied on a string around her waist—she wouldn't give him the one that might let the mystery out of her cherished superstition. Curiosity raised his voice. "There can't be any connection between death and peanuts, for heaven's sake." But she offered no explanation, meaning that it was one of those things you accepted on blind faith.

"Nat!" hollered their mother. "You and Molly stand by the crawl space and yell at your father. And keep yelling. I'm going for Tim Flynn!"

Something was terribly wrong. Her mother never yelled. Nat had already jumped up and gone with Lena following close behind, the back door slapping after them before Molly could think.

She ran out and stood behind them. Nat was on his hands and knees in front of the crawl space. "Dad, are you all right?" he hollered. "Dad . . . say something!" He started into the opening and she thought about the python. It might be living down there—that's what Willie had said when she'd heard about it. Under there. Then Tim Flynn's big hand moved her aside and grabbed Nat's scuffed black loafers.

"Come out, boy," he said. "Let me have a go at it."

"I can get him."

"No, son. On out of there!"

Nat shimmied out backwards. Tim Flynn couldn't fit in there, big as he was, and Molly was scared, more scared than she'd ever been.

He stuck his head in the opening and popped back out again, yelling in his deep voice that seemed to come out of a canyon.

"It's gas. Turn off the gas!" he yelled. "Ma!" he shouted at Mrs. Flynn who was coming in the gate. "Ma! Get the big wrench. Quick." Her eyes were popping. She turned and walked fast, then trotted, her feet crunching the gravel of the driveway, the chrysanthemums on her dress bouncing, the blue sweater flapping behind her like a cape.

Tim Flynn kept hollering. "Jim Flanagan! For Godsakes man, wake up! Jim Flanagan!"

Her father had eaten peanuts when he'd read his poems. "Some late visitor entreating entrance at my chamber door; This it is, and nothing more." The poems were full of dark shadows and suddenly Molly wondered if her father missed his own father so much that he would want to be with him in Hell.

She felt heavy, like wet sand. She tugged at Tim's sleeve. Her thoughts had left her speechless, but finally she blurted, "Mr. Remmler. He can move houses!"

"Shut up, Molly," said Nat. Big Tim wasn't paying attention anyway. He was clapping his hands to rouse her father.

"He can do it!" she yelled. "We could all get a jack and jack up the house and carry it off of him." They wouldn't listen and anyhow now it all sounded stupid.

"Jim Flanagan," hollered Tim Flynn. "It's now, man." He didn't pause for breath. Molly was breathing hard for her father, her heart pounding, and her mother was holding her shoulders and biting her lips, now red and about to bleed.

"Elizabeth, you're all at risk. Step away," Tim said to her.

But her mother didn't go. She stood there in a daze.

Mrs. Flynn came back with Tom and the wrench and Big Tom stopped at the corner of the house, found the main, and turned off the gas.

Then her father moaned like an animal from its lair, and tears fell down her mother's face but she was not crying out loud, just pouring quiet water from her eyes.

"Let me drag him!" Nat yelled into the face of Tim Flynn, but Tim ignored him and said "*Now* Jim. Come *now*."

And then more groans. "Tim, you?"

"Tim. Yes, Tim," yelled Tim Flynn. "Turn around, man. Look to the light."

"Get a flashlight, Nat," ordered Tim.

Nat ran wildly into the house, a boy so red-faced he looked about to explode. He almost knocked Lena down, but she sprang back up like a jack-in-the-box and said, "Don't worry Miz Flanagan, he's coming on now, I feel him coming on out."

Her mother hugged Lena and the two of them clung to Molly

as Big Tim kept urging, and the voice of her father would say, "Tim, you. Tim, you." Each time it would get a little closer and then Nat came back and held the light, waving it around by the crawl space in little circles. "See the light, Dad. See the spot." It reminded Molly of her first-grade reader and she laughed and cried and her mother didn't understand, but didn't say anything and neither did Lena because they were all crying out loud now. Frances came in the gate with that big giraffe, Ludie Finch, right behind her, and Tim Flynn yelled at them, "No smoking. No smoking, do you hear?" He glared at Mrs. Finch. But Frances Mahon reached up and patted Ludie Finch's shoulder and said, "Ludie'd do no such thing."

"James Flanagan, come on out, man."

"And play?" He was laughing. "Baseball. Third down and three to go." He was laughing hard. "You're out." His voice sounded crazy and Molly was afraid. She couldn't think of anything and stood there like one of her Grandaddy's cows, dumb as hell, worthless and without good sense. She tried to think of something really big and Byrd's stories ran through her mind— heads of martyrs rolling like cabbages, exorcisms of the devil— none of it practical, not even Willie's Bible stories, the parting of the Red Sea, or the miracle of Cana. She needed a miracle for *now*. If she could just remember the magic Latin prayers, but they melted in her hot brain. Religion was a pool of liquid as useless as warm milk.

Alfred moved beside her, holding her hand with his muddy little paw. "There's a butterfly," he said, pointing at a yellow and black Monarch. "He didn't go to Mexico like he's suppose to."

Even now, in the midst of disaster, he was a genius. She squeezed his hand. Her heart was breaking.

Charlotte and Jane stood by the gate in their tap shoes, neither one dancing. Jane's brother, Ray stood behind her and the little Finches, Jimmy and Sue. They peered from between the legs of their older brother and sister like criminals behind bars. All were silent.

George squeezed through the huddle, ran over and bent down to the crawl space. "Jim, get the hell out of there, man. Or I'm coming in to get you."

"George . . . no spitballs," her father slurred.

Mrs. Finch's long arm reached into her big pocket. Molly thought she was going for the cigarettes, that she'd sneak and light one and the whole neighborhood would blow! She heard herself screaming. And Nat shook her. "Stop it, Molly," he hollered in her face. It was only the beads Mrs. Finch was after. The flow of Hail Marys came steady now, smooth and swift from her barely moving lips.

Miss Doyle and Mrs. Flynn stood beside Mr. Remmler, all three holding hands.

"Mr. Remmler!" Suddenly she thought they might listen to the old man. "Tell them we could move the house!"

He opened his mouth, but before he could speak her father's red-gray hair appeared through the opening like a cocker spaniel in a doghouse doorway. Big Tim Flynn grabbed him by one arm, George the other. Nat was hovering. "Clear away now, folks," ordered Big Tim. "Let the man breathe. Everything's okay."

They dragged him out, and her father's eyes rolled in his head. They propped him up, but he could hardly stand.

"Amen," said Lena. "Amen."

"Drunk as a coot," said Ray Finch, sounding proud. He was probably just glad it wasn't his own father drunk for once.

But it was the wrong thing to say. Nat boiled over. "He almost died, you shitass!" Nat never said "shitass" in earshot of anyone but Molly, so the word startled her mother. "Drunk!" yelled Ray. Ray *was* a shitass. Nat ran toward Ray Finch and punched him in the face, sending him sprawling to the ground. Ray got up and Nat hit him again and Molly was glad for it. And glad she hadn't asked Nat for his chair on her birthday.

George ran over and grabbed Nat before he could hit Ray again. "Go on home," he said to Ray. His nose was bleeding like a streaming red bayou.

"I want my money," he said staring at Nat.

"What the hell money," Nat hollered back at him. "You're as crazy as a shithouse rat!"

George shoved Ray toward the gate. "Go on home, son. I mean now!"

"I'm going to get it!" shouted Ray, but he was backing and stumbling out the gate. "You better get home, Jane!" he yelled. Mrs. Finch followed him, clutching her rosary. She never said any of the things that mothers were supposed to say, such as "Everything's going to be fine, dear," or any of that and left all of it up to God. A woman in church had a rosary made like a bracelet and Molly thought how she might see about getting one for Mrs. Finch.

Molly had seen Jane smile when Nat hit her brother, but when Ray hollered about the money she'd looked plain scared.

The Flynns and George ganged around Nat and made silly conversation to calm him down. She guessed that was what friends were for. Mr. Remmler had socked one hand into the other when the fight started and seemed disappointed that it was over so quickly.

Frances said, "Elizabeth, call me later if there's anything I can do." She seemed to understand that it was time for all of them to go. She shooed Sue, Jimmy, Jane, and Charlotte out of the yard.

"Take care of yourself, Frances," said Elizabeth Flanagan. "You hear?"

Walking away, Tom Flynn had his mother on one arm, his aunt on the other. Mrs. Flynn and Miss Doyle were talking about how radiator heat was so much safer. "Floor furnaces are a danger, you know," said Miss Doyle. Mrs. Flynn seconded. "Babies fry on the grates all the time. Terrible burns they get on their little legs. Like link sausages. Whoever thought up floor furnaces ought to be shot."

"Sometimes these new houses blow up!" said Miss Doyle, looking relieved to have escaped the disaster of living next door to an exploding house.

"I told you all about the shells, now didn't I?" Lena was still shaking.

Molly's mother fanned her father with cardboard, taken from one of his shirts inside, as she listened to Lena.

"Pecans is all right," Lena persisted. "But don't you be letting him eat any more peanuts. They'd be the death of him yet."

Molly didn't understand how Lena connected peanuts with the furnace, although she did not doubt any of it. Mostly, she felt as though all of them were actors in a movie. Supposedly God watched over and directed them, but plainly He wasn't doing much of a job when He'd let things get so close to a bad ending.

Nat stood in back of the glider, pushing it. He looked white as a cloud, and floating. At first Molly thought he was scared, but Tim Flynn said Nat had inhaled too much of the gas. He tried to get him to sit down, but Nat stubbornly refused. Then Tim Flynn gave up on Nat and turned his attention back to her father, saying that if he'd been face down, instead of up, he would have died. Mr. Remmler said it was all "fate" and went on home.

Sitting on the glider with George beside him, her father was talking out of his head. The two of them probably knew as much about one another as a person could know, most likely all manner of secrets. Her father wanted a "fire" instead of a match, but George wouldn't let him smoke, even though the smell of gas wasn't much in the yard now.

"Nat, what was all that business about the money?" asked George.

Nat shrugged his shoulders, locked into silence about Jane and the Holy Ghost only knew what else. Keeping secrets, storing them for later use, she thought, was an art in this world of talkers.

For a while they all stood around under the darkening sky, the sun low and nodding, the chilly day rolling into the cold of a November evening. Like brown cows in winter without much grass left to eat, they were waiting for someone to rescue them from this world.

Chapter SIXTEEN

Rataplan, rataplan—on a black horse she rode through the meadow, the amber grass waving in the wind—rataplan, rataplan, rataplan—straddling bare-legged, she clung to the thick mane, her velvet cloak billowing behind her, the sky red-hued and flashing, and, letting go, she woke suddenly to the rhythm of her own hard-beating heart. Rataplan. Rataplan. Rataplan. Rataplan.

For a moment she thought the room was her own, the familiar blue-gray fluorescence of night when time was the same as space, stretching endlessly into the unknown. The smallest sound meant life and she listened hard so that her ears pulsed and rang with the strain.

When the door opened, a white form floated into the room, crisply bright against the haze of blueness. The water felt cool going down. Molly merely nodded, imagining herself a soldier wounded in battle and unable to speak. Then she was left alone in the blue chamber. The eye, she thought, and suddenly she knew it was blind.

She remembered the striped mask coming down on her face and struggling mightily against its smothering force. Now she reached for her face and felt the bandage—at least she had not died. But she dared not cast her voice against the silence or breathe the air that filled the room, afraid she might waste what life it held.

Her father was not there—most likely he was outside some-where, pacing back and forth. Her mother was not in the room either and for this she was surprised.

Her heart was beating slow and steady now—like a metronome, she thought. Under the white cover she felt her elbows, her wrists, then pressed her fingers along her ribcage—*do re mi fa*. Up, then down. *Fa mi re do.* A blanket of drowsiness came over her, the room wavering, the bed rocking like a cradle. Her head was a for-tune-teller's ball and within it she played a grand piano in the midst of a garden, pressing with all her strength, the keys com-mitting no sound. All around her the flowers sang.

THE NEXT thing she knew, her parents and Nat were standing beside her bed. "You came through, angel," said her father. He seemed uneasy in the presence of her bandage and she wanted to tell him that it wasn't his fault, just like it was not his fault that his father had left the world before his time. Her mother was smiling. She had been on edge for days before the opera-tion, saying little, and now looked quietly pleased.

Nat said, "I'm going to miss that old eye. Talk about a slip-pery character. Never knew where the . . . Sam Hill it was going." "Hell" was what he'd meant to say.

"Certainly had a personality all its own," said her father. "I'll remember it long and well."

None of them had ever said much about the eye before. Now they were delivering its eulogy. Was it blind?

"For now you have to lie still," said her mother. "But in a few days you'll be coming home, the doctor says."

"You're to wear a patch when they take off the bandage," said her father. "After it's completely healed, you'll wear the patch on the other eye. You have to work Old Rover to get the muscle strong. After that, you'll be just like everyone else."

This she doubted. No one was like anyone else.

"She's still drowsy," her mother said. "Molly, just drift off now. Everything's fine. We're going upstairs for a minute. Nat'll stay with you."

"You're going?" That they would go off and leave her just barely alive was plain heartless. But she was hearing the pitiful sound of her own voice and didn't much care for that, either.

"We won't be long," her father said. He was tall. About as tall as a man should be. But standing there at the foot of the bed he looked a little stooped. "George checked Frances into the hospital this morning," he said, his voice faltering. He didn't seem particularly happy about this.

"The baby's a little early," said her mother. She looked sad now—sad that she didn't have a baby of her own, Molly guessed. "She's on the floor right above you. George's up there seeing her now."

Her father opened the door and stood aside, holding it for her mother. He lifted his shoulders slightly as if he'd had something more to say, then decided against it. When he shut the door Molly heard their footsteps in the hall, hollow sounds that dimmed to faint echoes.

Nat was sitting in a chair beside her bed. He ran his fingers through his hair. Like deep water it parted, then lapped over itself, dark and shining. "There might be some problem with the baby. They ought to have gone on and told you. You'd know it soon enough."

"They never tell me anything."

"You're Dad's angel, for Christ's sake," he said. "He doesn't want you to worry about anything. And both of them think you're just a kid."

"And you don't?"

"Half kid." Then he thought better of it. "Three-fourths when it comes to the piano. God *damn* why don't you just go on and get the 'Tarantella' down."

"I'm no good at piano," she said in a pitiful tone that was in itself an embarrassment, but here she was wounded—probably the eye was bleeding under the many layers of bandages—and still having to defend herself. "Maybe I'll just play the scales in the recital."

"The doctor said your eye is going to be just fine. It won't be roaming all over hell and back anymore so you ought to do better. For Christ's sake, nobody expects you to go on stage."

"Easy for you to say. You're going to be an actor . . . a famous movie star!"

"Priest," he said. "I'm going to be a priest." He looked startled, almost afraid. Most likely he'd never said it out loud before.

She didn't know what to say and just looked at him with the one eye. She felt clumsy, like a Cyclops. Still, she could see better than before. "What about the cursing . . . you just plain cuss all the time. Even if nobody hears you but me. And when you're *not* cussing you're always *about* to." She pictured him standing in the pulpit wearing purple vestments, raising hell with the sinners, flailing his arms, telling them they were no damn good. Then she thought about Jane. "Besides, you're in love with Jane. And you stole Ray's money."

"Damn. Where'd you get all that?"

"Did you steal Ray's money?"

"Jesus Christ . . . no. Ray started an avalanche when he hollered that. I must have loosened a screw or something. A lot of his customers asked me to collect. They were sick of trying to keep up with the back bills. Besides I wanted my pay for sub- bing for him. He'd go for damn ever without collecting. Always stalling. His father would bail him out when it was time to pay his paper bill—but then he'd rough him up bad. Ray would promise to collect on time the next month, but Old Man Finch was always gone off somewhere or drunk and Ray would never get around to it. Too busy worrying about what he had on his mind. Anyhow, after I collected the money, I'd always give his part to Jane, but I didn't know she was using it as a bribe."

"So Ray wouldn't bother her?"

"You're finally catching on. She couldn't bring herself to tell anybody—just couldn't say it and she made me promise not to say anything either. Not one word. Anyhow, when I gave her the money, she kept it. When he found out later—that I'd collected from his customers—he threatened to go to Mother and Dad and tell them I'd stolen the money, but Jane played him, said if he went and told them or anybody else she'd tell what he'd been trying to do to her. She promised him she'd talk me into giving him the money back and he believed it. She was just buying time. But he was impatient even though he was scared stiff she *would* tell on him, afraid Old Man Finch would beat the hell out of him if he knew."

"So what did she do with all the money?"

He started laughing. "That's the good part. She spent every last penny of it on her dancing lessons. But after Ray was flapping about the money, George started asking questions—he was afraid we'd have another fight. I told Jane she'd have to go on and tell her father. No matter what."

Molly thought of Nat having to carry Jane's problem around for so long a time. And of Jane now having to say it. She pictured the words clotted in Jane's throat, choking her—then spurting like blood from a wound.

Something about laying up in a hospital bed loosened Molly's tongue and made her go on and ask all that had been sitting inside of her. "But how can you be a priest if you love her? You do love her, don't you?"

"Sort of . . . I guess so," he said. "But not enough to move me away from what I've come to. It's hard to explain. But nobody knows, so keep your mouth shut."

His secret was safe with her. She would guard it for however long he wished. But she thought of what lay ahead of him, such a long, hard way. At the same time she figured he was lucky, knowing as he did, what he wanted, what he was meant to do.

She watched him lean back in his chair and stretch his arms out from his sides. She wondered how it would be, having a priest for a brother and all. One thing she knew. She'd never confess to him. Not even the smallest white lie. She knew he'd just cuss her for sinning.

"Grandmother Willie and Grandaddy Bob were here while you were under the knife. Willie kept on about how she didn't believe in tampering with the work of God. As soon as they knew you were out of the operating room and in recovery, they went home. She left this for you."

Willie's message was scribbled on a piece of crumpled notepaper that Nat handed to her after he'd smoothed it. The crinkles looked as the lines of a map. *St. John 5: 39. Search the scriptures: for you think in them to have life everlasting. And the same are they that give testimony of me.*

The handwriting had a nice rhythmical flow, but Molly wasn't sure what St. John, or Willie for that matter, had meant by this and she felt too fuzzy to think of it now. She folded the paper and set it aside. Fuzzy or not, she knew now that she was not blind. A kind of "Amazing Grace" or something.

Byrd had sent a vase of red roses, and an evocation from the martyr St. Thomas More: *The devil it is therefore that, if we for fear of men will fall, is ready to run upon us and devour us . . . therefore when he roareth out upon us in the threats of mortal men, let us tell him that with our inward eye we see him well enough and intend to stand and fight with him, even hand to hand. Remember, Dear Molly, that the psalms will sustain you through each and every one of life's trials.*

Molly remembered it was St. Thomas More who'd said the psalm "Miserere" just before the executioner beheaded him with one stroke. What this all had to do with anything she didn't know. She pictured Byrd and Willie as two old lionesses fighting over one piece of meat. Maybe she'd start up her own religion. With no saints and no Bible. No hymns. There'd be no sack cloth, nor ashes, no martyrdom. They would sit cross-legged in the dirt, circled around a roaring bonfire, and all play harmonicas and sing some simple tune. Maybe "Buffalo Gals."

Nat had grown tired of sitting and was pacing back and forth, pausing to look out the window. "Second Street's right over there," he said. "Dad and George's old stomping ground."

While the nurse checked her pulse and temperature, her mother and father came back into the room. Molly waited for them to say something about Frances, but they did no such thing. Her mother carried a present wrapped in white paper and tied with a red bow. "An early Christmas gift," she said. "We didn't think you should have to wait this year."

Molly unwrapped the package, discarded the bow and Christmas paper, and opened the box. Under the several folds of tissue paper that crinkled as she moved it aside lay a marionette, a minstrel man wearing a purple coat studded with gold buttons, an orange bow tied around his neck and, on top of his head, a white straw hat.

"Closest thing we could find to Punch," said her father.

"Punchinello," she said.

She'd seen little black girls with white dolls, but never a white girl with a black doll. Of course this wasn't a doll at all—she was far too old for such things—but it did seem peculiar, having this nappy-haired black marionette with a smile like a slice of watermelon. She felt the hair soft as lamb's wool. The whites of his eyes were half-moons around deep-green irises centered with black pupils. "I was going to make a marionette," she said. "But this is much better than anything I could ever do."

"You still can make one when you feel up to it," said her mother.

"Lena's got that one all planned," said her father. "She's set on go for Moses. Soon as you get home."

"How is Frances?" she asked, feeling the marionette's hair.

"Fine," said her mother.

Her father nodded, as if to reassure himself, then quickly changed the subject. "Before I forget, there's something I've been meaning to say. I'm declaring the python officially dead. You might call it a decree." The message delivered, he sat down.

"Gone from these parts," said her mother, talking from somewhere out of her childhood.

Molly wondered why they brought up the python when she hadn't thought about it in days. And they didn't seem to understand the real problem with snakes—that they came into your life without invitation. And stayed as long as they wanted. "What do you think happened to it, really?"

"Down river," her father said. "Probably in Greenville by now. Or Natchez."

"In Lick Creek," said Nat. "Liable to come out any time, any place." He had assumed his diabolical expression, one foreign to his face. He couldn't hold it for long.

"Your play's over, Nat," said her father. "Molly's been talking in her sleep about snakes again and I want it to stop. Logic has it that in cold weather a python wouldn't hang around. The creature of legend is playing to a new audience. In warmer climes. *I said.*"

There he went again, trying to protect her. Didn't he know it did no good, that around this corner or the next, whatever was out there, sooner or later she'd bump into it? She saw everything clearly now. Like Lick Creek, evil ran all over town—on the surface, in the bayous and sometimes underground. Whether or not you understood it or saw it, always it was there.

Chapter SEVENTEEN

On her second day home from the hospital, Molly was sitting on the purple corduroy bedspread. The germicidal lamp hanging on the closet door shone pale blue in the bright sunlight slanting into the room.

"You don't have to do that, Lena," she said. The ivories and ebonies were pearled and glossed from Lena's polishing. The John Thompson was opened to the "Tarantella."

"Just making sure everything's ready," said Lena.

The piano recital stood waiting on the other side of Christmas, just a couple of weeks away. She must practice—she knew that, but for a short time each day she was allowed to leave off the patch and was stalling, just staring out the window, marveling at the fine lines of the world.

She focused her eyes across the street where Alfred was digging in his yard. Bud stood beside him, watching intensely as if Alfred were an archeologist soon to unearth a significant find. In a week's time he'd managed to pock the yard like a gopher. A pattern of holes was taking the shape of a huge star, like the board for Chinese checkers.

Nat came in with a cup of hot chocolate, carrying himself like a waiter wearing a stiff tuxedo, and handed her the cup. "Don't expect this again," he said. He looked out the window at Alfred.

"Poor guy," he said. "He's been king of the hill and now he's got to share with a baby."

"Nobody ever said what they *named* the baby," said Molly.

"They were thinking of Merlin, after George's father, but they've changed their minds . . . and I don't know now," said Nate. "The baby's retarded. A mongoloid."

"You mean . . . like Ronnie Rosemary?"

"Not that good, I don't think."

"So that's why no one's been invited to see the baby," said Molly.

"Essie says he's real cute," said Lena. "He's a marked child all right. Jesus's own sweet one."

Molly pictured Ronnie Rosemary as a baby in a crib, how he might have looked then, the short flattened skull, the slanted brown eyes almost oriental. She thought of Frances holding the imperfect child, George looking over her shoulder, pretending that he was proud. She wondered if George passed out cigars. She doubted they'd tell Alfred that his tiny new brother was going to die at the age of fifteen.

Nat took out his collection book and marked the date on the page. "I'm off," he said, and left the room.

Lena unrolled the butcher paper, then got down on the floor and prepared to finish up a sketch of Goliath. The day before she'd drawn the small David with his arm drawn back ready to hurl the stone. Standing on the sidelines, in the midst of the onlookers, Lena and Molly held bags of rocks for David. As always, they wore the white robes, but instead of blue glasses, Molly wore her black eye patch.

When she was done with Goliath, Lena said, "This afternoon—if Miz Flanagan don't mind, that is—we'll start on Moses."

"Great," said Molly. "But I've got something to show you first." She waited for Lena to finish rolling up the paper. After it was placed back in the closet, Molly picked up the box beside the bed, opened it and pulled out the crossbar. The marionette dangled from the strings. "I haven't named him yet," she said. "I thought you might come up with one." The wooden head nodded, and the shoulders, arms and hands wavered in a loose jiving rhythm.

Molly hadn't expected Lena to be offended by the marionette. "Black man's got strings enough without you poking fun." She held one hand in the other. Her jaw was set firm. "I don't like that. I don't like that one bit. No ma'am, not one bit. If I was to name him it wouldn't be no Christian name. It wouldn't be that."

"But you told me about the Rabbit Minstrel Shows. How you went there when you were a girl and how you loved the dancers." Suddenly the one eye seemed to blur, just like before the operation.

"That's some different. I don't know exactly why, but it's so. Maybe back then I just didn't know no better. Besides, white folks have no notion of black man's ways. You don't know nothing about none of it. You hear?"

"He's not real or anything."

"He's real, all right," she said. "Real low-down."

Lena rearranged the house keys dangling from her waist and retied her apron strings very tight. "I'm for the kitchen now. The dishes need doing." The keys jangled like her voice as she left the room. Her footsteps seemed to pound through the house.

The marionette's smile looked overdrawn, like someone who laughs too long at a bad joke. Molly put him back in the box and covered the face with tissue paper.

She sat down at the piano and played the C major chords, then the "Tarantella." At the end of the piece she placed her hands in her lap and sat very still. The house was quiet. Whenever she practiced, everyone scattered—not even the ghosts hung around —the only sound the occasional bouncing of a tennis ball coming from the living room. She heard it now—thumpety-thump . . . thumpety-thump. Lena had been the only one able to withstand the assault of mistakes. And now, not even her.

Molly took the marionette from the box, trying to understand Lena, but as she held it, looking at the fine, bright expression, the button nose, the hands that were slender and well formed, the green irises that reflected her own face, she couldn't get her mind off of Frances. How she would feel about God playing such a dirty trick.

When she heard the knocking at the window, she turned to see Alfred's eyes peeping at her from just above the sill, his hair curling up from beneath the ribbed stocking cap. She guessed he was now permitted to cross the street without assistance. Either that or the Mahons had their hands full with the retarded baby and hadn't noticed.

Alfred's cheeks were splotched a bright red, his chilled breath fogging the glass. She opened the window slightly. "I have to practice." Alone was what she thought, but didn't say it.

"Can I come in?" he asked.

"Not now," she said.

He kept standing there, not giving up. "Merle cries all the time," he said.

"Babies do that," she said in the sure way of someone who'd had first-hand experience. "You're calling him Merle?"

"I do," he said. "And Essie does. Essie takes good care of him. She's rocking him right now," he said as he teeter-tottered from his toes to his heels, back and forth. "Mother and Dad just call him *the baby*. I think it's because he looks funny."

He looked sort of dopey himself with his head all bound up in the bright green cap, his big blue eyes swimming in the cold air. "I've already got your Christmas present," he said.

Right now she didn't really want his company, but just closing the window seemed cruel. "You can come in and turn the pages if you want to," she said.

With a big grin on his face, he stuck his arms straight out from his shoulders and flew around the yard like a bird. He stopped dizzily on the front steps, and entered the house, clumping through the hall to her room. As he looked over her shoulder, his head cast a green shadow upon the keys. With her eye patch and his shadow she felt strangely like Long John Silver with the parrot. "I'll tell you when," she said.

"Okay." He took off his jacket and dropped it on the floor. He rubbed his hands together, warming them, then nodded to her like he knew what he was doing. He took his duty seriously, standing very straight. "Ready," he said solemnly, and cleared his throat. He pointed one finger toward her face. "Now."

As she looked at him she thought, Toscanini?

Chapter EIGHTEEN

"How come you never play this one's song?" Alfred was pointing to the composer's picture on the music book. "He looks like the man in the red suit."

"Why can't you just call him Santa Claus, like other kids?" Alfred was becoming more and more of a pest. Each day he would show up to turn the pages. Even today on Christmas Eve, he'd come into her room carrying a small gift and, setting it on top of the piano, had shifted side to side, until finally she'd asked him to sit down. "Anyhow," she said. "That's Peter Tchaikovsky."

"I don't believe in the man in the red suit, if that's what you think. I saw Dad putting my toys under the tree last year."

It was irritating how his leaps into life were so swift. She had taken much longer to find things out. Peter Tchaikovsky did look quite a bit like the Santa Claus in *Miracle on 24th Street*. She decided to try playing "Waltz of the Flowers," but only the treble clef. She was familiar with the melody; the bass she would just play in her head.

"It sounds better than the other one," he said after she'd finished a few bars. She allowed him to bang for a few minutes before she turned the page to the "Tarantella."

"You're giving me another book for Christmas, aren't you?" he asked.

"Maybe," she said. "I haven't finished wrapping. And I have to practice now." In truth the old Burgess she had planned to give him was sitting there on the shelf in plain view. But lately it was becoming more and more clear that he'd already outgrown talking animals. She considered giving him the marionette instead.

"Whatever it is—and I'm not saying what—you'll get it in the morning like always. You can't open it until then, anyhow."

"If you went on and gave it to me now," he persisted, "I'd have something to do in the middle of the night when Merle cries. I'd have the pictures to look at."

This was reasonable, but she ignored him and played the "Tarantella." She played it three times over. Alfred refrained from holding his hands over his ears.

A SHORT time after Alfred was sent home, a car stopped in front of the Finch house. Mr. Finch and Ray got out and went inside at the same time the Flanagans were backing out of the driveway, heading to the Hardy house for the annual Christmas Eve dinner. Everyone in the neighborhood now knew that Mr. Finch had taken Ray away from home for the protection of Jane. Each of them saw the Finches, but said nothing. Nat was driving; soon he'd be sixteen and no one talked when he was driving anyhow. Her parents spoke only when the car came to a red light, falling abruptly silent as soon as the light changed to green and the car pulled forward. Molly wanted them to talk about Jane and what they thought about Ray Finch being in the house again. But she knew they would not discuss it in front of her. She began to look out the window.

This was her first time out of doors without the patch. She had on her new tortoise-shell glasses. The crisp angles of houses, the curving branches of trees, the roundness of traffic lights—the strength of ordinary things, that was the difference. The eye saw more clearly with each passing day, but while the outside world took on shape, certain other things—nameless feelings—remained limp and fuzzy. The marionette hung in the closet out of Lena's sight. Molly hoped that once Alfred had the minstrel man, the offence standing like a wall between Lena and herself would crumble.

Molly had unrolled the butcher paper that morning, waiting in anticipation, but Lena had quickly run the dustmop in and out of her room. She had barely spoken, saying only, "Miz Flanagan thinks drawing the Bible's a waste of time. I'm not up to it nohow."

Her gift to Lena was under the tree, a blue scarf that was almost silk. Now she knew it would remain there, until she herself placed it in Lena's hands or put it away.

Nat pulled in front of the Hardy house, scraping the tires on the curb before stopping completely. Her father managed to hold back comment. Her mother coughed.

The wreath on the door was pine and holly, the profusion of berries and cones dusted with white snow from a spray can and encrusted with glitter, but somehow the house on Madison looked more dreary than usual in the cold grayness of a winter's early evening.

Her father looked at her. "Last year of coloring Christmas, angel. Your mother's going to ask Willie to retire your Crayolas when you turn thirteen. Maybe she'll put you in charge of the punch or something."

His message of hope was as grand as any gift, but her mother neither confirmed nor denied this, just glanced at him and walked on up the steps, carrying the covered dish.

Inside, the house was crowded with the Hardy family, the aunts, uncles, and cousins. From a black string thumb-tacked to the mantle hung a shining gold star, twirling in the stirring of air as Nat closed the door. Everyone watched as the Flanagans entered. "Merry Christmas" went round the room, then their eyes settled on Molly's to see how the operation had turned out. Embarrassed, she looked only at the star.

"Glad it's all over, Molly," said Uncle Bob Roy. The other uncles, Al, Luke, and Clement, all agreed. "Worth the money," said Uncle Luke.

She refused to look up, but wondered if any of them had guessed where the money had come from.

"Bet you were scared," said her cousin Howard, sticking his fourteen-year-old face forward, probing. She did not like the attention anymore than she liked Howard. The other cousins, Albert, Thomas, and Luke, Jr., had the good grace not to ask questions.

On the hearth just below the star, silky strands of angel hair—salvaged time and again from Christmases past—enclosed the manger scene like spun ice; Jesus, Mary, Joseph, their donkey, the shepherds, sheep, wise men, and camels stood on the snowy cotton batting, glistening characters in a cold fairy tale.

Her father and Nat sat down with the men and boys. When

President Eisenhower came on the television screen to deliver his Christmas message, everyone quit talking, except Grandaddy Bob who hadn't yet talked anyway. The president didn't sound or look particularly merry. Her father had said that after Eisenhower traded his general's uniform for a business suit, he never again seemed truly alive.

Along with Bob Roy's wife, Aunt Ida, Aunts Emalene, Willene, Jesse, and Ella W. bustled about in the dining room, setting platters of turkey, dressing, ham, and a variety of relishes on the table covered with red cloth. In the center was a gumball tree created from the branch of a sticker bush and painted silver with poisonous paint. No one was allowed to eat the red and green candy. After nodding to Grandaddy Bob, her mother went to the dining room and in between the turkey and the dressing set down the bowl of tuna.

Earlier, her father had suggested that they go on and eat Christmas dinner—"whatever is served"—rather than upset Willie and Grandaddy Bob with the Church's rule about abstaining from meat on Christmas Eve. "You know that the four of us sitting there eating tuna fish spoils the whole meal for them, El. They regret each and every bite. For us to have a piece of turkey on Christmas Eve can't be as much a sin as *that*." But she wouldn't hear of it, and had gone on adding sweet pickle relish to the tuna, coating it heavily with paprika.

On the top shelf of the bookcase the limbs of the little tree strained with the burden of glowing lights, ornaments, and silver icicles, the whole of it veiled with more of the angel hair. Nat smirked as she took her coloring book and the crayons from the shelf and grudgingly went into Willie's bedroom where the other granddaughters were already coloring robes and togas. The last time, she thought. And then never again.

On the floor in front of the small fireplace, Marsha was hard at work. As always, her picture was near perfect. "Your eye looks okay to me," she said, looking up. "I thought you'd have a big bandage."

From the sound of her voice Molly could tell that Marsha thought the eye was only an excuse to delay the recital, that Molly hadn't practiced, hadn't been ready, and wasn't ready now. "The doctor said I could leave the patch off for Christmas Eve," she said. "After that I have to wear it for a while longer." She was cross with herself for offering the explanation.

"The recital's in January," said Marsha. "In just two weeks."

Her voice, weak and impalpable, was nonetheless a threat. But Molly was eased some by the knowledge that Marsha would be coloring Christmas until 1957. "I'll play with or without the patch," said Molly.

"Well, if you don't know your piece by then, Grandmother can always play along *with* you. Like she did last year."

Molly had yet to get through the "Tarantella" without stumbling and lately had become sick of the sound of it, but right now she yearned to play the thing over and over again. She was sorely tempted to tell about Byrd's offering to send her to the Conservatory, but after picturing herself in a mob of jeering cousins when she failed to be accepted, she committed herself to a vow of silence.

In the true spirit of Hardy dedication, the other cousins were busily coloring and barely looked up. Sarah and Rebecca colored lightly, tinting the robes, huts, and landscapes in delicate pastel colors; Miriam outlined each figure, leaving the color of the centers up to the imagination, while Louise—her crayons worn to nubbins—pressed down with a strength that made her picture even darker than the *Angelus* hanging above them. Miriam was almost twelve; Rebecca, eleven, and Marsha, with a birthday two days after Christmas, nearly there; Sarah was ten, and Louise, nine. They all talked of school, friends, and Sunday school and of what they wanted for Christmas.

Molly was in the same barnyard, yet always looking from the other side of the barbed wire fence, a gosling older and wiser, she thought, but isolated in her own pen, away from the ducklings. But all of them, even Marsha, seemed as anxious as she was to get done with coloring Christmas.

President Eisenhower concluded his message. The droning persistence of his voice in monotone had seemed as long as a sermon at midnight mass, but without the fire of Monsignor's dramatic inflections.

Now from the dining room came the sound of Uncle Bob Roy tuning his old fiddle. Always the fiddle fractured all conversation. Her father had said he doubted Bob Roy could get in tune even with a Stradivarius, but always there was the hope. He had captured his audience and wasn't about to let go of it. The good thing was that on Christmas Eve Bob Roy sawed only simple tunes—"Away in the Manger" and "O Little Town of Bethlehem," leaving the more complex "Turkey in the Straw" for some other family gathering, possibly a spring night when they could open the windows for relief. But right now, listening to the bow scratching across the strings, she worried that at the recital she would sound as horrible as Bob Roy.

Nat made faces at her from the living room, rolling his eyes, lifting his shoulders with each faltering note. At the same time her father, Grandaddy Bob, and the uncles and cousins grimaced and blinked their eyes. But now and then Uncle Bob Roy played a note pure as gold—Molly could almost see it stretched out in the air—and she thought if he kept on playing, someday all his notes would be golden.

Marsha chattered away. "I've got 'Minuet in G' for the recital," she said loftily, as though she'd caught a falling star. "Mother's making me a hoop skirt with a bustle."

Aunt Ella W. would always come up with some scheme. Last year she had dressed Marsha in a Mexican serape and sombrero for "La Cucaracha." Marsha had played the tune with the invariant sound of a Mexican jumping bean, not much expression for sure, but she didn't miss a single note.

"Spinning Song," said Sarah, shrugging and looking defeated. "Well, somebody has to play it." Always she was a good sport. Rebecca said, "Musette" and looked self-assured. Miriam had finished outlining her picture and was packing up her crayons. The others thought the shortcut unfair, but Miriam had long since established her own style, one that Willie seemed to accept. Miriam had chosen "Prelude" by Berens for the recital, but only the first part—a series of chords in moderato, flatly refusing to follow it with the second movement, the Allegretto, which would have filled in the blanks. "I'm not wearing any costume, either," she said firmly.

Molly loaned Louise her crayons, since her cousin's had all but worn away. Wisely, Grandmother Willie had placed Louise with the "Toreador Song," so she could play as loud and hard as she wanted.

Grandmother Willie came into the bedroom, collected the books and inspected each picture. "Molly, there you go again giving red hair—you know it wouldn't have been red. Well, at least you stayed in bounds." Joseph's hair was on fire, but at Christmas Willie was somewhat more forgiving. She commented on each picture, then led her troupe of granddaughters to the table.

The rigors of an active religion were too much for Grandaddy Bob, so Uncle Bob Roy took his place as head of the family and said grace. While Bob Roy dawdled over the words, stringing them into an off-the-cuff sermon, Grandaddy Bob refused to bow his head or even pretend to pray, instead glancing proudly at his grandchildren and at his own daughters. Probably God never noticed Grandaddy's withdrawal from the Methodist Church anyhow, as quiet and unobtrusive as he was. She wondered what they would all say—what Grandaddy Bob would say if anything—when they found out that Nat was to become a priest. She wondered if they would let *Father* Nat bless the food and if so, would they then eat any of it?

The line formed around the table and stretched into the kitchen, the Flanagans toward the end. By the time they got to the bowl of tuna, it was empty. "Don't say a word," said her father in a low voice. "Eat the sweet potatoes."

The potatoes had a pallor more palish pink than orange. Molly remembered Willie's saying that iris tubers were "just about the same as sweet potatoes" and whispered a warning to her father and Nat. "I don't know for sure," she said, "but it looks like Grandmother's gone and boiled the iris tubers."

"I pass," said Nat.

"Where's your sporting blood, son?" said her father. "Eat hearty. Both of you. Iris or whatever's in the bowl, and the rolls and relish. And over there," he motioned to the other side of the table. "The candied apple rings."

But her mother either didn't hear him or didn't want to. "Mother," she said to Willie, "we brought the tuna because we are not allowed to eat meat tonight."

Willie was behind her in line and about to spear a piece of ham. She coughed and put down the fork. Not only did Elizabeth Flanagan not fit in with her own family, she wasn't making any attempt to pretend otherwise. Not even on Christmas Eve. It almost seemed as if she was trying to be different for its own sake.

"Quite a spread, Mother Willie," said Molly's father. He was going for a spoonful of the dressing.

"Giblets in that," snapped Elizabeth Flanagan. "And renderings."

Grandaddy Bob forgot his manners and scratched his head with his fork. "Renderings is in most everything on the table," he said, somewhat dismayed. He helped himself to the green beans laced with bits of ham.

Skim it off, maybe." That was Willie's advice, but she knew it wasn't any use. She sighed and left her plate almost bare of food.

"Not to worry," said Molly's father. "There's plenty to eat. It's all gorgeous." He was scooping up a shimmering spoonful of red Jello from the molded ring. "Bob Roy," he said cheerfully, "after dinner, how about a round of 'Dona Nobis Pacem'?"

AT HOME Nat brought in the logs and her father started a fire. Molly was relieved to be home. At Willie's she had felt stiff as an icicle and was only just now melting. She wondered if her mother ever would. Molly put "Adeste Fidelis" on the record player and plugged in the tree, but before the colored water in the bubble lights beaded, two carloads of aunts, uncles, and cousins drove into the driveway.

Nat was pulling down the shade. "It's Aunt Nellie, Uncle Joe, Aunt Rose Kate, Uncle Pep, and all eleven of the animals. They're coming here first."

"They can't visit the Mahons this year," said her mother. "Not with what Frances is going through."

"Unholy tribe," said her father, swallowing his bourbon. "Not even a grace period. Barricade the icebox! Man the flanks!"

"They're all another year older," said her mother. "Maybe it won't be so bad as before."

"That's what I like to hear, El," said her father. "Faith in humanity. But honestly, how'd you arrive at *that*?"

"They can't behave badly all their lives."

"They can and will. As much as I love Nellie and Rose Kate, I hope they won't stay long. Brace yourselves."

The tribe of eleven boys were off and running immediately while Nellie, Joe, Rose Kate, and Pep were still getting out of the cars. The boys stampeded across the yard and charged into the house like a burst of cannon.

"Merry Christmas, men," her father said. He didn't attempt communicating with these nephews by name. Instead, he whistled, snapped, and pointed. "The kitchen is off limits, men."

Molly heard the thump of a cane. If they'd lived in the right era, these nephews might have made a pretty fair gang, she thought—if someone could have gotten them under control.

When Aunts Nellie and Rose Kate and their husbands came into the house, her father set the time limit right away. "We're going to midnight mass," he said. "How about yourselves?"

"Last year, we got kicked out," admitted the oldest boy, Tip. The boys pushed and shoved each other, jabbing elbows. "Father Murphy said for us not to come back. Ever."

"Somehow that doesn't surprise me, Tip."

"I'm sure he didn't mean forever, Tip," said Molly's mother, attempting charity while moving the antique oil lamp from a table to the mantle.

Together the cousins filed toward Molly's room like segments of a centipede. She followed, just watching them, staying well clear of their elbows. They were fascinated with the eerie blueness of the germicidal lamp; they called the room Mars. Without asking they opened the closet door and pulled out the box of blocks that her mother was supposed to have given away long ago. They tumped it and built the Great Wall of China in record time. Then they formed an eleven-man band with one instrument, Molly's piano, all of them fighting to play it at once. The result was the sound of war and she imagined them in a recital banging out "The 1812 Overture" or "Ride of the Valkyries," bombs dropping all around. United, they pressed all of the notes at one time, an achievement of horrors, then, famished from the concert, they headed for the kitchen. "Grub," said Tip.

Molly looked in the living room. Pep and Joe couldn't keep up with their wives, Rose Kate and Nellie. Joe was asleep and snoring. Pep downed his last drink, then stood and announced that it was time for all respectable families to be in their own homes. He went outside, got in his car and leaned on the horn.

"Sounds like he means it," her father suggested. "Best to head on home."

"And spend Christmas Eve alone, with *them*?" said Rose Kate. Making the rounds, both Rose Kate and Nellie had consumed more bourbon than either of them could properly tolerate and now started to reminisce about the Christmases of their childhood. Nellie described the sumptuous meals, the elegant decorations, the crush of visitors.

Elizabeth, what was it like out in the country?" asked Rose Kate, just being polite.

"It must have been quiet out there," said Nellie. "You all had candles on the tree, I'll bet."

Neither Rose Kate nor Nellie understood that Elizabeth Flanagan took such questions as criticism. "Some candles were on the tree," she admitted. "But everybody knows the house had electricity. It was as modern as any." On the settee between Rose Kate and Nellie, her mother was goldenrod in a bed of wild roses.

Nat was busy standing guard at the kitchen door, repulsing

the invasion of cousins. They went back to her room, wrecked the Great Wall, rebuilt it all over again, and then discovered the marionette hanging in the closet. "A nigger puppet," said one of them, laughing.

The others jeered and said curse words worse than Nat's. She stood in the hall and looked in, afraid of what she'd see.

They shook and jiggled the marionette, fighting over it. The little straw hat was first to go. It got stomped on the floor. Then the bow tie and coat were ripped to shreds. "Stop!" she shouted, but the din of voices was a *movimento* at once loud and invincible.

The cussing finally moved Nellie and Rose Kate to action. Nellie called her horde of villains to the car. Rose Kate's bunch fell in line and followed them.

The naked marionette lay on the floor, a dead man mauled in a riot. Nat came in and shook his head. "Ten years, they'll all be in jail."

Molly was tired and on the brink of tears. She had not found much pleasure in the marionette. Still it was hers and not something to be laid waste by a bunch of hoodlums. But she guessed that Lena would be glad.

WHEN THEY left for midnight mass, Mr. Finch's car was still parked on the street. "I'm surprised at that," said her father. "I suppose he and the boy are staying the night."

She was last in line as they marched down the aisle in church. It had already been a long night and she felt like a zombie sleepwalking. From the pews the faces glowed, filled as they were with the spirit of Christmas, and everyone in church was smiling. Molly thought, as the music swelled, how the Holy Ghost was a spirit for *all* time, not just this one season when everyone was full of joy and hope that would fade as the hours ticked away. The Holy Ghost didn't promise happiness, so the loss of it—like when something happened that was terribly disappointing—didn't start you wondering if there *was* a Holy Ghost like it did with God or Jesus. Instead, the Holy Ghost was there inside you opening up small windows so you could understand what in hell was going on, as Nat would say or however much of it you could take in at one time. She'd not yet taken in Grandfather Nate.

AT HOME, just before she was ready to slip into her bed, she heard the frantic voice of George Mahon from the living room. "I don't know where in hell they could have gone. The door was locked, so they weren't kidnapped."

"Of course not," said her father. "Who would steal a . . . baby?" He'd almost said "retarded baby."

"We were only gone a few minutes. Ludie called. She was hysterical. Finch beat up Ray bad. The boy ran away. Alfred and the baby were both sound asleep. We didn't think leaving for a few minutes would matter. Anyhow, Ludie called the police on Finch, but when they got there, she wouldn't press charges. The boy was hurting the little one . . . Sue. Now the police are out looking for Ray. Tom Flynn's one of them. When Frances and I got home, Alfred and Merle were missing. Vanished."

"Let's go," said her father. "Nat, you too. They can't have gotten far."

"I'll wait with Frances," said her mother. "Molly, stay here in case the phone rings."

Molly unplugged the Christmas tree. It didn't seem right to leave it on. She wandered through the house and into her room. She sat down at the piano, fingering the keys, not really playing anything. Alfred's fear of them taking Merle away was far greater than she'd understood. Why else would he have gone off in the dark with Merle like that? And then she thought of Essie. "Essie takes good care of him," Alfred had said. She pictured Alfred loading Merle in his red wagon, hauling him to Essie's. And she remembered that neither Lena nor Essie had a telephone.

Quickly she left the house and walked across the street to the Mahons'. Up the steps and onto the screened porch that was faintly lit, she looked around for Bud, careful not to startle him, but the dog wasn't there. She was feeling for the doorbell when through the lace curtain she saw her mother and Frances talking soul-to-soul. Her mother wore a look of sympathy. The two women were holding hands, Frances crying softly. At that moment Molly felt a gladdening pure and shy as a white violet. She decided not to disturb her mother's chance for friendship.

She walked quietly across the porch, down the street, and around the corner toward the wooden footbridge that Lena and Essie always walked over. The bayou water was a narrow stream now, slow moving in its advance toward the river. She saw a dark figure down in there against the concrete embankment. She knew he'd also seen her. Just then the feeling came over her like when something chased her in her dreams. The bridge moaned as she ran across the wooden planks.

She darted across Jackson Avenue into the dark street of Anchorage, not knowing which house belonged to Essie. Lena would know. In front of Lena's house she realized the late hour—at least two o'clock. And here she was, a white girl in the middle of the night in the pitch blackness of Klondike. She saw herself on the front page of the newspaper, dead on the sidewalk with a knife stuck in her chest. She drew a deep breath, pulling in life.

The light was on in Lena's house. Up finishing the Old Testament, she thought. She knocked loudly at the door. Instantly, Lena's black eyes peered through the window. The door locks clicked—there were four, the reason for the many keys.

"That you, baby?" The chain held tautly. "What in this world. My Jesus." She unlatched the chain, reached out, grabbing Molly by the arm, and jerked her into the house. "What on earth is you doing out in the night, Molly? What you doing out there, girl?"

"Alfred ran away with Merle. I think he took him to Essie's."

"Lord have mercy," she said. "They ain't at Essie's. Essie ain't there herself. She and all the chirrens gone off to stay the night with her grown daughter. Clear across town."

If not there, then where?

"Your Mama and Daddy are going to be out of their heads," she said. "You ought to have that head of yours looked at. Got to get you on home. You don't even have on no coat."

Molly hadn't even thought about the cold, but now she was shivering. Lena went to find coats for both of them.

On the walls of her tiny living room, the baby Moses hid in the bulrushes. Beside him, Molly, wearing the black patch, carried the water jar. Lena was fanning Moses.

I'm going to get me a ladder," said Lena, her arms now full of coats. "I'm scarce running out of room, so the ceiling's next. It's going to be some harder, though."

"Maybe I could help you," said Molly, slipping on the brown wool coat that had been her mother's.

"That might be of some good," she said. "But your Mama won't allow any such thing."

"The marionette's ruined," she said. "The cousins went wild. They tore him up."

"I'm sorry," she said. "I was going to say I was sorry about being mad at a little old wooden thing with strings. I don't know what got into me. Maybe we'll fix him if he's not too far gone."

"I've got your present," said Molly. "It's a scarf. Blue."

"Blue is real nice."

AS THEY crossed the bridge, Molly saw the man's figure reflected in the water below. Lena saw him, too, and held her finger to her lips, linking her arm in Molly's. He walked toward them, smoking a cigarette, the tip of fire deepening as he took a drag. Molly shuddered inside Lena's warm coat. The silhouette became Ray Finch, holding a knife in his hand. He stopped and lifted his head. She thought he recognized her. She heard the sizzle of his cigarette as it hit the water. He passed under them and started running eastward, toward the far bridge, and from it she heard the sudden sound of thudding. Then dark figures appeared in a cluster. "Halt! Or I'll shoot!" Ray Finch didn't hear the warning or didn't care. He kept on running toward the men. "Halt or I'll shoot! Throw down your weapon!" The voice was

Tom Flynn's. "Halt or I'll shoot!" Molly kept looking over her shoulder as Lena pulled her on across the bridge. Just as Ray Finch veered, disappearing into the black opening like a bear into a cave, the shots rang out.

She and Lena were running fast now, down the street and around the corner, not stopping until they hit the door of the Mahons'.

"LORD GOD, where have you been!" Her father was beside himself. Her mother's face was streaked with tears. She held Merle in her arms, swaying back and forth.

"They're shooting at Ray Finch," said Molly. "Down in the bayou!"

Her mother passed Merle to Frances, and then hugged Molly. They all circled around: her father, Nat, Lena, Frances, and George. Merle was round and pink like any other baby, but the difference was that he'd always be one, Molly thought, and never worry over what he couldn't change, or feel things until his heart got shattered, and never get mired in deep trouble the way Ray Finch had done. Then she saw Alfred standing in the doorway, yawning, holding his pillow. Beside him Bud looked just as sleepy. And then Tom Flynn burst in. "He got away. We fired a warning and he ducked into one of the culverts. It's too dark to find him now."

"Lordy, what you people done gone and done to Christmas. And Alfred, where'd you go off to with the baby?" Lena was purely exhausted.

"I woke up and everybody was gone. I was scared. Me and Merle and Bud spent the night in the basement."

"We didn't think to look down there," said George. "Alfred laid Merle on top of the sheets in the clothes basket and made himself a pallet. When Merle woke up and cried, Elizabeth heard him. Some watchdog, Bud—he never even barked, was snoozing like the baby."

BEFORE SHE would let her father drive Lena home, Molly insisted on giving her the present. They crossed the street and entered the house. Molly plugged in the tree, the lights like jewels in the darkened room. While Lena opened the package and tied the scarf around her neck, admiring it, Molly's mother whispered something to her father. He went to their bedroom and then handed an envelope to Lena, the same sort of envelope in which the rent money was always placed. "A Christmas bonus" was all he said.

A look of suspicion crinkled Lena's brow. "I best not ask where this come from," she said. "There's folks across the way could stand some help. What I don't know won't hurt me."

As they were leaving he said, "And how—may I ask, dear Lena, is the mural going?"

"Just a job, Mr. Jim. One of those things what eat at you until it all gets done. That's the way of things when you got to get what's inside you worked out, if you know what I mean. Like Molly here learning piano. It's just a job."

Molly knew it wasn't so. She understood about Lena's art, putting the hope that was down inside her up on the wall. But it wasn't so about the piano playing. If playing the piano was her job, she would have been fired long ago.

Chapter NINETEEN

On Christmas morning, while sitting in his favorite chair, reading the agricultural news, Grandaddy Bob slumped over and died. His was a message never delivered, a gift still in the wrapping. At his request, he was placed in a pine box that remained closed at the funeral home and buried without ceremony. Willie looked saddened, but she cried not one tear that anyone ever saw. Grandaddy Bob's death did not postpone the recital.

IN JANUARY, on a bitter cold day, Molly wore her red corduroy bathrobe as she practiced the "Tarantella" three times without looking at the music, stumbling only twice. She then slipped into the wool skirt that almost fit, blue-and-green plaid, and put on her blue sweater. She wore the turquoise ring that Nat had given her for Christmas, the second coming of Byrd's gift. (Jane confessed to him that when she urged Molly to pitch the ring in the grass, she had picked it up herself and slipped it into her own pocket. Later, needing more money for the dancing lessons, she'd hocked it.) Nat had retrieved the ring from the pawn shop.

Ray Finch had not been found. Molly didn't know about Mr. Finch—he'd never been around that much—but Ludie Finch sorely grieved for her son, pacing the porch, praying the rosary for him most every minute of each day. If Jane danced her way to stardom—whirling on stage in a dress of lavender silk, receiving a bouquet of pink roses after a stunning performance—Molly doubted Ludie Finch would rise above sadness long enough to share the moment. For she must have imagined, as Molly herself knew, that Ray Finch was living underground in Lick Creek, on grubs and worms.

MOLLY SAT on the end, lined up with her cousins in the row of chairs. The parents and brothers sat in rows behind them. She wore a corsage of red roses sent by Byrd. She was more simply dressed than the others in their taffetas, silks, and satins— Louise wore red, Rebecca blue, Miriam green, and Marsha the yellow hoop skirt, but Molly was the only one with flowers. The yellow hoop skirt was troublesome from the start, curving out in front, threatening to pop up over Marsha's head. Molly helped hold it down in self defense.

Sarah was sick, so the "Spinning Song"—always somebody played it, always it was first—was noticeable in its absence. Miriam went first with the Berens. She played it curtly, was over and done without flair. Two times Rebecca played "Musette" perfectly, the second time because she'd enjoyed herself so greatly the first. Then Louise got everyone's attention with the "Toreador Song." Like a bull, her fingers pawed and stomped at the keys.

Aunt Ella W. had underestimated the narrow alley between the chairs of the pianists and the bench itself. Marsha's skirt was a foot wider than the space. Molly wanted to get her own piece over and done and was nervous during the wait. It took the efforts of three aunts to get Marsha up from her chair and seated at the piano. With her hair all done up in corkscrews, Marsha really looked like a protegé of Beethoven. She played well enough, though the audience, fearing the skirt would spring forth, was distracted and uneasy.

Then it was Molly's turn. She quickly took her seat on the bench and got on with the "Tarantella." Trying as she was not to miss the notes, she felt as if she were playing it in slow motion. Certainly no one could dance that slowly without falling asleep, but she missed not a single note. When she finished she heard Nat and her father clapping louder than necessary.

Grandmother Willie seemed quite thrilled. "Molly, since you're the oldest, why not play another piece?" Willie was looking nostalgic and Molly guessed what came next. "We haven't heard the 'Spinning Song' yet. The recital won't seem the same without it."

If only through the illness of Sarah, Willie was having it her own way, but she took to giving concessions. "Would you like to look at the music this time?" Not waiting for Molly to answer, she opened the book and stood to the side. "Press the pedal if you want." Her generosity was overwhelming.

Molly took her at her word and decided to do both things— press the pedal and follow the notes—and when she got well into the piece, she loosened up and got rolling. Instead of plowing over mistakes, her notes sounded clear and ringing, the rhythm of the spinning steady and strong. Her face flushed with